Hunters & Co.

I0586982

JB HELLER

HACKER HEART—HUNTERS & CO. BOOK 2

Copyright © 2022 by Author JB HELLER

Published by- Author JB Heller

Cover Design by- Tall Story Designs

Editing by- E.R. Whyte

Formatted by – JeBDesigns

Chapter One

Belle

HAND OUTSTRETCHED, I WIGGLE MY FINGERS AND cackle with glee. "Pay up losers!" My sisters grumble and bitch me out under their breaths, but they all give up the goods. I smile as I tally my winnings.

"Are you seriously counting it?" Snow grouses with a scowl.

"You're just sore because I won. You all thought the dean banging both Neil's mom and his girlfriend was far too scandalous for a little town like Shiloh

Springs. I can't believe you're all so shocked. Small towns are where it's at."

Ariel eyes me from across the booth. "But the dean isn't even good looking. I don't get the appeal."

I shrug. "Probably boredom on the mom's part and likely something to do with grades on the girlfriend's end."

It's Friday night and we're crammed into a booth at Jack's Bar and Grill. Our baby sister Kida took in her last skipper and handed in her resignation from the family business this afternoon. We're celebrating her new career path.

But it feels kind of weird, like it's not something we should be happy about.

Keeds isn't cut out for our line of work—not many are. Bounty hunting is a tough gig that requires skill and coordination. While she has the skills, she's severely lacking in the coordination department. Most of the skippers Keeds has apprehended—or more accurately incapacitated— have involved an accident of some description.

Yet, somehow, she never ended up being the one to sustain the injuries. Her targets, however, weren't so lucky. Personally, I think it's a gift. One time, she was about to cuff a perp and he yanked his arm out of her grasp, making her stumble. Somehow her taser went off, nailing the dude in the balls.

It was absolutely brilliant.

Sitting opposite me, she's picking at her nail polish and it's making me twitchy. I place a hand over hers, then wait for her to meet my gaze. "What's up?"

Keeds swallows, then glances at our other sisters before licking her lips and saying, "Do you guys think I'm a failure?"

My brows furrow, and I shake my head. "Of course not."

"Why would you even think that?" Meg—the oldest of the five of us—asks.

Snow throws her arm around Kida's shoulders and gives her a little squeeze. "You feeling sorry for yourself again? I thought we'd been through this. You're a badass, end of story. Who cares that your methods were…unorthodox. You still got the job done most of the time. Nobody has a hundred percent success rate."

"Yeah, but I quit. I'm giving up."

"So?" Ariel puts in, leaning an elbow on the table to peer around Snow at Keeds.

Meg clears her throat, drawing our baby sister's attention. She gives her that look, the motherly one that grates on my nerves. We had a mom, an incredibly amazing one. Keeds needs us to be her *sisters*, not wanna-be replacement moms. But Meg didn't get that memo.

"Honey, did you even like being a bounty hunter?" Meg asks.

Keeds swallows hard, then gives a weak shrug.

"No one expects you to be anyone other than who you are. No matter what direction that takes you in, we'll always be there, and we'll always be proud of yo—"

I roll my eyes as I cut Meg off and squeeze Keeds hand, bringing her focus back to me. "You're going to be a kickass baker, do you hear me? Screw what anyone else thinks. And you know what, if you decide later that you'd rather be the one eating the cakes instead of baking them, that's cool too."

She grins at me, then nods. "Okay."

I mentally pat myself on the back for putting that smile on her face. She worries too much about what we think. All Keeds has ever wanted was to be just like us older girls, but we take after our father, and she takes after our late mother. If klutz was a gene, they both got it.

I'm sad she couldn't find a place where she fit within Hunters & Co., but happy she's willing to give something else a try. And with her slightly disturbing obsession with cheesecake and doughnuts, I have no doubt she'll be an amazing baker.

Finishing the dregs of my beer, I reach toward the jug for a refill, only to find it empty. I glare at my sisters. "Okay, who emptied the jug? You know the rules, last one buys the next."

Snow snorts. "That's *your* rule. Our rule is she who comes up dry, must replenish the well. Looks like you're up."

I groan, "But I'm wedged in the corner."

Meg wastes no time sliding off the end of the bench seat to let me out. She even sweeps her arm with a flourish as she says, "Not anymore."

I shuffle across until I can stand. "Thanks," I mutter, then stalk through the crowd to the bar, waving down Jase when I catch his eye. He lifts his chin in acknowledgement then reaches under the bar for a fresh jug before filling it to the brim.

"Anything else while you're up here?" he asks when he reaches me.

Why not? It is Friday, after all. "Five shots of Jameson, please and thank you."

Jase grins. "Comin' right up."

Valentine

OH, MY GOD.

Walking into Jack's tonight, the last thing I expected to see was the love of my life on top of the bar dancing her ass off in six-inch heels.

Yet here I stand.

"Pick up your jaw, son, you're drooling," my dad says from beside me, a smug grin on his stupid face.

I snap my mouth closed. "What is she doing? How did she even get up there on those stilts?"

"Jesus, not again," my coworker, Kline mutters from behind me.

I shoot him a quick glare over my shoulder. "What do you mean, *again*?"

Kline being the uptight asshole he is, ignores me. He remains stoic as he pushes into the crowd, making a path as he stomps toward the bar. I follow behind him, making use of the route he's cleared.

When I reach the bar, my gaze is drawn up a pair of long, toned legs encased in skin-tight black pants. I peer up at the most beautiful woman in the room and she does a weird little booty shake slash squat thing, smiling down at me.

"Hey!" Belle yells over the music from the live band. "Come dance with me!"

My eyes widen as she latches onto the collar of my shirt, tugging me forward. I wrap my fingers around her slim wrists. "Let's not and say I did," I call up to her.

She frowns and shakes her head back and forth, sending her blonde ponytail swishing around her like a cat o'nine tails whip. It slaps me in the face, and I wince. But she's oblivious and still trying to tug me up onto the bar with her.

"Val, you never dance with me!" she whines.

"How much whiskey have you had?" Kline asks her.

She giggle-snorts.

Dear god, she's tanked.

Which I kind of already knew but Belle snorting is the most un-Belle thing in the universe. She'll die if she finds out she *snorted*.

"Okay drunky, let's get you down," I say, sliding my hands from her wrists to her elbows, then higher. "Come on, before you break your neck up there."

"Pfft, there's literally nothing I can't do in heels. Who do you think you're talking to?"

"A very drunk girl whose coordination is likely compromised..."

She arches a brow and stares at me. I take advantage of her moment of deliberation, tugging her toward me. She falls into my waiting arms with a high pitched squeal that rings in my ears. But I don't even care about the possible damage to my eardrums because she's wrapped around me like a python, and I love it.

With her face pressed into my neck, she groans, "Dick move, Val."

"Sorry Bee," I murmur into her honey and vanilla scented hair. I'm not sorry, not even a little bit. But she doesn't need to know that.

"You good with her?" Kline asks.

I'd forgotten he was there. Turning to face him, I nod. "Yep."

He grunts something unintelligible, then turns back to the bar and waves down Jase.

Belle lays her head against my shoulder as I cradle her against my chest and make my way toward the exit. The crowd parts, allowing me through because I'm holding one of the infamous Hunter sisters. They're practically royalty in this town. Everyone knows who they are, and how unwise it would be to piss them off.

The girls are fiercely protective of each other, so

when I reach the door, I do a quick survey of the booths. I spot the others crammed into one at the back, and Kline has already made his way to them. I assume he'll tell them I've got Belle if they didn't see me take her.

By the time I get to my car, Belle has completely mellowed out. Her mouth is practically brushing against my throat. The little puffs of air caressing my skin send a shiver down my spine.

I clear my throat. "Gonna put you in the car now, Belles."

She sighs and tightens her arms around my shoulders. There's zero space between her enticing curves and my upper body. I take a deep breath, mentally shaking the lustful thoughts from my brain, and refocus on the task at hand.

With skill that can only come from growing up as the unofficial protector of a bunch of girls when they're drinking, I open the passenger door one handed then deposit her inside. Once she's safely secured, I round the hood and slide in behind the wheel. Belle rolls her head to look at me, a sultry smile playing on her lips as she reaches across the console and places her palm on my thigh.

I freeze. Belle is an exceedingly affectionate and horny drunk. Always has been. I'm glad she doesn't overindulge too often because I don't think I could handle it more than I already have to. Not when I know she's only touching me because she's plastered.

Taking a calming breath, I throw my car in gear and pull out of the lot. Thankfully, nothing's farther than a ten-minute drive around here, and I pull into Belle's driveway before her palm has ridden up too high. When I get out, I take a quick second to rearrange the goods, then go about getting her out of the car and into her house.

Once we're inside, I kick the front door closed behind me, then slip out of my shoes. Belle's weird about footwear. Striding down the short corridor off her living room, I take a left into her bedroom. It's pristine, with not a thing out of place, as always.

It's a warm night, I figure she'll be fine to sleep atop the covers, so I don't bother pulling them back before depositing her gently on the mattress.

With an outstretched hand, she beckons me closer. "Don't go, Val."

I give her fingers a quick, reassuring squeeze. "I'm right here."

A small sigh slips from her parted lips. "Stay," she hums.

My dick is all about that idea, but there's no way in hell I'd ever take advantage of a situation like this. Keeping my mouth shut, I move down to her feet, slipping off her fire-engine red heels and taking them to her shoe closet.

She had major renovations done on the house when she bought it a few years ago. She had the attached bathroom downsized to expand the walk-in closet, and the spare room next to the master converted into a walk-in shoe shrine. That's what I call it, anyway, because I'm sure most women don't own this many pairs of shoes. And if they do, I don't think they display them like this.

I turn in a circle, examining all the shelves for where this particular pair lives. I can't for the life of me work it out, so I put them on the fancy ottoman thing she has in the middle of the room. She can sort it out tomorrow.

Reentering her room, my mouth goes dry, and my heart takes off at a gallop. I stare at the tight black pants and frilly pink top she *was* wearing when I removed her shoes. They're now on the floor at the foot of her bed. I firm my jaw and tell my dick to calm the hell down before things get even more uncomfortable in my jeans.

"Come to bed, Val," Belle murmurs.

My name from her lips when she's practically naked...it's too much. I refuse to look. I can't. Keeping my gaze averted, I stride for the door. "I'll stay in the guest room, okay? Call out if you need anything," I tell her as I go.

I'm across the hall and locking the door behind me in record time. Leaning against it, I close my eyes and reach for my throbbing dick, giving it a hard squeeze.

I am not, under any circumstances, going to jerk off. Nope, not going to happen.

I have superhuman self-control. Getting off to thoughts of Belle when she's drunk in the other room is not cool. I've been in love with Belle Hunter since I was sixteen years old, I've flogged the log many a time with thoughts of her front and center. But never in her house—that'd be pervy and weird.

And I am not that guy.

Then my hips punch forward all on their own and my palm flattens over the hard ridge behind my zipper.

Down boy.

Now is not *the time.*

Gritting my teeth, I straighten away from the wall, tug my shirt and jeans off then flop face first on the mattress and pray she doesn't try to pick the lock again...

Chapter Two

Belle

Rolling to my side, I groan as sweat breaks out across my forehead and a wave of nausea rolls through me. My temples throb as I gingerly sit up, and I'm pretty sure someone drove an icepick through my brain while I was sleeping.

Or maybe it was that bottle of Jamison's? Things are a little fuzzy.

I squint at my nightstand, a note along with a bottle of water and two white pills sit waiting for me. *Valentine to the rescue, once again.* I smile despite how disgusting I feel and reach for the pills. Popping them in my mouth, I wash them down with a hearty swig of water before picking up the note.

You snore like a chainsaw when you're drunk. Take the aspirin, then have a shower. I'm in the living room depleting your coffee stores and obliterating your high scores.

-Val

Just knowing he's here makes me feel a little bit better. His presence has always had that effect on me. I fold the note in half then slip it into the top draw of my nightstand. I'll put it with the others later.

I take a deep, fortifying breath, then force my ass out of my bed. I stagger to my little bathroom, and groan again when I catch sight of myself in the mirror. I'm a straight up trainwreck.

Val is the only person on earth who gets to see me like this. Not even my sisters have seen me at my worst. Val promised me a long time ago he'd always have my back, and to this day, he's never let me down.

I flip on the shower, then strip off what's left of the clothes I was wearing last night. I feel so gross, but the second I'm under the hot spray, I begin to feel a little more human. For a long while I just stand there with my eyes closed and face tipped up into the downpour from the rainfall showerhead.

Eventually, I reach for my face wash and scrub yesterday's makeup from my skin then go about my usual morning routine. Fifteen minutes later I'm fresh as a daisy and strolling out to join Val on the couch.

His head turns my way when I step out from the corridor, a smile playing at his mouth. "Morning. Coffee's on the counter. How you feelin'?"

"Grateful," I tell him, backtracking to the kitchen. He must have made it while I was in the shower because it's steaming hot and in my favorite mug. I wrap my hands around it then bring it to my lips to blow on before taking a sip. "Mmm, so good," I murmur.

I shuffle over to the couch and curl up in the corner, tucking my feet under my butt. My eyes flutter closed, and I sigh happily as I inhale the lifegiving aroma wafting from the mug cradled between my palms.

"Should I give you two a moment alone?" Val asks.

My eyes pop open, a glare at the ready, but the grin on his handsome face wipes it away before I can unleash it. I roll them instead. Which isn't smart, as the movement causes a spike of pain to ricochet through my head, making me grimace.

Val leans over, placing a hand on my arm. "You okay? The aspirin not working?"

"Not yet. If the caffeine doesn't make it kick in, I'll take some Tylenol."

He nods, then sits back, turning his attention back to the TV and the controller in his hands.

"How long have you been up?" I ask.

"I don't know, an hour, maybe. Went in to check on you, and you were still out cold, so I had a shower and helped myself to your fridge. Speaking of, you hungry?"

"That would be a negative. I reckon I'd throw up anything I ate right now."

He eyes me for a moment, then says, "All right. Let me know when you change your mind. Maybe dry toast or something."

Val is unbearably gorgeous *and* impossibly sweet; he's a double threat. It astounds me he's single. Not that I mind; I'm actually pretty damn thankful for it. It means I get him all to myself. His girlfriends never like me, and that usually ends up causing issues for both his relationship and our friendship.

Thoughts of his last girlfriend Maggie and the ultimatum she gave him creep into my brain, and I just know I'm pulling a sour-ass face right now. I didn't like her from the beginning, but to be fair, I rarely like the women he dates.

But this one—she was something else. Right from the get-go, she made it very clear she didn't care for our friendship.

They'd been dating for seven hellish months when she pulled the *it's her or me* card. I wanted to rip out her unflattering hair extensions and kick her insecure ass. I mean, who even does that? Children, that's who.

"You okay? You're awfully tense over there," Val says, side-eyeing me.

I give him a stiff nod. "I'm fine. My head's just sore."

Which isn't technically a lie. Thinking about that chick makes me stabby at the best of times, let alone when I'm fighting a hangover.

"Time for some Tylenol." Then he's tossing the controller aside and marching to the kitchen, where he raids my medicine box.

Forcing thoughts of Maggie and her manipulative ways out of my head, I wriggle deeper into the couch cushions. Val returns a minute later with two pills and a fresh glass of water. I refuse the drink in favor or knocking them back with my coffee. We fall into a comfortable silence as he goes back to playing The Legend of Zelda and I sip on the remainder of my coffee.

———

THE WEEKEND PASSES TOO QUICKLY—PROBABLY because I spent it laying around binge watching The Umbrella Academy with Val—and the next thing I know it's Monday morning and it's back to the grind.

As is my way, I'm ten minutes late when I walk in the door. I stroll over to my desk, boot up my computer, then turn on all three monitors. I've just hit twenty-nine and not once in my life have I been on time for anything. Nobody so much as lifts a brow when I eventually make my way into the breakroom joining the already in-progress weekly meeting.

There's a free spot between Meg and Kline, *hard pass*, and another next to Valentine at the end of the table. I slide into it, and he snags a glazed doughnut and napkin for me without me uttering a word. "Thanks," I whisper and Val winks but says nothing, seeing as Dad is addressing the room and handing out assignments.

I break off a piece of my doughnut and pop it in my mouth, careful not to mess with my lipstick. It melts on my tongue, and I barely hold back a moan. Val stiffens ever so slightly beside me, and I side-eye him. He shrugs me off, so I go back to devouring the deliciously sweet and sticky pastry.

These babies are the reason I bust my ass at Trick's Gym several times a week. And it's totally worth it.

I'm just licking the last of the icing off my fingers when the meeting wraps up. I wipe my hands on the napkin Val had given me, then wash them at the sink for good measure. Food is not allowed anywhere near my computer. Food brings ants, and ants are creepy. They also create problems nobody wants to deal with if they get inside your processor.

Snow sidles up to me as I'm drying my hands. She stands there staring at me with a smirk on her blood-red lips until I snap, "What?"

"Looked like poor Val was about to burst a blood vessel watching you eat that doughnut," she says, leaning her hip against the little kitchen counter.

This again. I shake my head and give her shoulder a condescending pat. "You're delusional."

She scoffs. "Pot, meet kettle."

Snow's been singing this song for years, and it's getting old. "He's my best friend. What don't you get about that?"

"Oh, I'm not disputing *that*. I'm just sayin' if more

was on offer Valentine would be *all* over it. I'm surprised he didn't pop a boner the way he was fixated on your mouth while you licked the icing from your fingers."

"He was not."

"Uh, yes Belle, he was."

"He really wasn't."

I would have noticed, wouldn't I?

Disbelief blankets Snow's sharp features then she throws her hands in the air. "You're kidding me with this shit, right? You are the smartest person in the room, Belle, and you can't see that guy is head over fucking heels for you."

I purse my lips, but nothing comes out. Val is my friend, my *best* friend, but he's not into me. That's a pipe dream I let go of a long time ago.

Snow frowns, then tilts her head. "I can't figure out if you refuse to see it because you don't want to acknowledge that you feel the same way, or, if you pretend not to notice because you like the attention. In which case, dick move, big sister. Val deserves better than that." Then she turns on her booted feet and stomps out of the room, leaving me alone with my tumultuous thoughts.

Valentine

THE SECOND MILLER WRAPPED THE MEETING, I WAS out of my chair and sprinting for the door.

Sometimes I'm not sure if I've got a filthy mind, or if Belle is purposely torturing me. I mean, come on—licking icing off her fingers? What man on the planet can see that and not have dirty, dirty, thoughts? I had to lock myself in the bathroom for a good ten minutes and think about dying kittens and hamsters with incurable diseases.

Back at my desk, I'm filling in some paperwork when I feel her presence enter the pit and as always, my gaze automatically drifts in her direction. Her brows are furrowed and she's gnawing on the corner of her bottom lip as she makes her way to her workstation.

My eyes stay fixed on her. Not five minutes ago she was in a blissed-out sugar high, and now she's… forlorn. *What the hell happened between then and now?* I'm still watching, and wondering, when Kline smacks me on the back of the head.

I spin around, glaring at him. "What the hell?"

He raises a brow but doesn't say anything as he continues to stare at me.

"You know normal people communicate through this nifty thing called *words*. And they string them together to create sentences. You should try it some time." I turn back to my computer; I don't have the time or inclination to decode Kline and his unique form of communication.

But it doesn't take long for my attention to wander back across the pit to Belle, and the downward slant of her normally smiling lips. Not much ruffles her feathers, so someone must have been a real dickbag to get under her skin like this.

After an hour of sneaking glances and not detecting any change in her mood, I push my chair out from my desk and roll across the room to her. She needs a distraction.

She lifts her head as I near, an infinitesimal upturn tilting the corners of her mouth. "What are you doing?"

"I'm pretty sure my laptop is either about to shit itself or it's got a virus. Mind coming around to check it out for me this afternoon?"

"You haven't had it that long; it shouldn't be dying on you already," she says. "Did you install the antivirus program I gave you when you bought it?"

I rub the back of my neck as my cheeks heat. "Umm, maybe…"

Her pink painted lips pop open in a perfect O. "What do you mean, maybe? You did or you didn't."

"I…didn't?"

"Are you asking me or telling me?"

I clear my throat and avert my eyes. "I tried but I screwed it up and I was too embarrassed to say anything."

"How did—actually, you know what? It doesn't matter. I'll come over after I finish here."

My smile is instant. "Thank you." Then I scoot my chair back across the pit to my desk, satisfied I've given her something to think about other than whatever was bothering her. I knew she'd jump at the opportunity to do this for me. There are few things Belle loves more than fixing computers and helping people.

She's so kind and generous; it's one of the things I love about her. She's always been this way, even though she—like her sisters—holds herself at arm's length from almost everyone. I can't even imagine what a force she'd be if she stopped holding back.

"A virus?" Kline says, suddenly appearing beside me.

My hand flies to my chest. "Fuck me, you need to

stop doing that. You're going to give someone a heart attack one of these days."

He rolls his eyes. "You been looking up dodgy porn again? I told you to just subscribe to a legitimate site after what happened last time," he announces loud enough for everyone in the pit to hear.

I gape, then shoot a glance over to Belle and find her staring at us with what I'm pretty sure is morbid curiosity in her big blue eyes. My head snaps back around and I scowl up at him. "What the f—"

Kline drops a hand on my shoulder. "I know you have some weird fetishes that most reputable companies probably don't cater to. But I'm sure if you look hard enough, you'll find one. You can't just be downloading random shit off the internet, no matter how much it tickles your pickle."

How he can say any of that shit with a straight face, I will never know.

I blink at him, my mouth still hanging open, as I search for something—any fucking thing—to save face. Because the string of words that just fell out of his mouth are utter bullshit. "Why, just… why?" I ask, bewildered.

"Really Valentine? This is not the place to be discussing your sexual proclivities," Miller's deep voice says from across the pit.

I spin in my chair to find the boss man standing in the doorway to his office, a disappointed frown marring his stern features. Well, shit. As if it wasn't bad enough that Belle is under the impression I have undesirable sexual cravings, now her dad is, too.

Shoot me now—like, in the foot or somewhere else unfatal—it'd be less painful.

Chapter Three

Belle

I LOVE MY JOB, I REALLY DO. BUT ALL I CAN THINK about right now is Valentine and whatever this *weird fetish* Kline was talking about could be. I'm smart enough to know that there's a good chance Kline was just being a dick, and he could have made it all up to embarrass Val.

But what if he wasn't?

A whole set of questions that I haven't allowed myself to dwell on in years come rushing to the fore. When I was young and naive, I thought Valentine and I might, maybe, possibly, one day, end up together.

I know better than to believe in the fairytale, forever kind of love now, though. I may have only been eight when my mom died, but I remember the devastation losing her caused my family. Especially dad. He and mom were two halves of a whole, and when she died, she took a piece of him with her, and he's never quite been the same since.

Because of that, I don't let anyone get too close, even friends. Not that I really have many outside of my sisters. I prefer my close, tight knit circle which barely extends outside of family.

The older I got, the clearer it became that a serious relationship was just not in the cards for me. I feel too deeply—I always have— and doing so will be my downfall if I let it. Friendship is all I have to offer. Anything more is just too dangerous.

Heaving a heavy sigh, I do my best to turn my attention to the emails on the screen before me. I mindlessly go through them, forwarding applications to Dad and Doc, as they're in charge of risk assessments, and so on. Unfortunately for me, nothing too exciting has come through.

I compile a few files for dad to review and distribute, then run a skip trace on a guy Snow found on the FBI's most wanted list. She used to find targets on there once or twice a year when she was bored, but ever since Ariel started dating Kass, she's been bringing me names on the regular. Every single one of them is on the run for crimes against women and children.

This guy... though... I don't like the look of him. I'm not sure what it is, but I know when to trust my gut, and this is one of those times. I complete the trace anyway, then save everything into an encrypted file before printing a copy out for Snow. After collecting the papers and arranging them into a folder, I go in search of the most rebellious of my sisters.

Valentine

I AM IN THE ZONE. HEADPHONES IN, KILLER inspirational playlist blasting, fingertips typing a mile a minute as the story appears on the page in front of me.

Few things feel better than when I hit my stride and the words just come to me without any effort. I can't wipe the smile from my face. I live for moments like this, just me, my apartment, my laptop, my tunes, and the world I created in my head. A world where I can be with the woman I'm in love with and give her everything she needs and wants.

It also happens to be a place where I don't pop inappropriate boners at work.

My pulse races as a fuck hot sex scene begins to play out...

Propped against the doorframe to our bedroom, I watch her sleep. She must have been exhausted when she fell into bed, since her skirt and blouse are pooled on the floor at the side of the bed, but her bra, underwear, and heels are still on. She didn't even bother climbing under the blankets.

I enter the room, intent on removing her shoes and tucking her in. At the foot of the bed, I place a knee on the mattress, lift one slender ankle and slide the deadly spiked heel free. She moans softly, and I caress her toned calf. "Shhh baby, it's just me," I assure her, then move to the next foot.

She is a sight to behold, her pale skin splayed out across the dark duvet, and long blonde hair still in a perfect twist against the back of her head. Once done with her shoes, I can't help but glide my palms up her gorgeous legs, pausing to cup her delectable ass and give it a gentle squeeze.

Another moan, this one wanton as she arches her back, pushing her perfect cheeks into my waiting hands. I squeeze them again, then dip my face to run my nose over her creamy flesh and inhale her scent. She's intoxicating. Everything about her sets my blood on fire.

I trace her panty line with the tip of my tongue, and she shudders out my name. I grin against her silky skin, then sit up and push one knee up and out to the side spreading her open for me. A damp spot appears on her underwear, and satisfaction fills my chest. So wet for me and I haven't even touched her yet.

Moving up her back, I plant my hands either side of her head, then murmur in her ear, "You want me, or sleep, baby?"

Her ass lifts, grinding up into the hard-on behind my zipper as she sleepily replies, "You, always you."

I kiss her cheek, her jaw, her throat, her shoulder, then all the way down her spine. By the time I reach her ass again, I'm so amped up I can't wait to be inside her. Sliding a finger into her panties, I tug hard, tearing the flimsy lace that covers her pink pussy.

She whimpers, her hips rolling, searching me out.

One hand on the small of her back stills her before I lose my mind, and I unfasten my pants with the other and free my straining dick. I slap it against her pretty ass once, twice, three times. She squirms harder under my palm, forcing me to lean my weight atop her to keep her in place.

"Patience," I grunt, hanging on by a thread. I wanted to take her slow and sensuous but she's pushing all my buttons.

She shakes her head against the pillow, eyes still closed, lips parted. "Fuck me, Val. Need you. Please."

Oh fuck, I can never say no to her. I part her cheeks, and my gaze fixed on the rose bud of her ass, bend and lick it. She quivers and rocks into my face again. I dip my tongue down farther, tasting her tempting pussy. My eyes fall shut as I lose myself in feasting on her body.

My dick's throbbing and leaking by the time I come up for air. I line it up with her entrance, then slowly sink inside her slick heat. She whimpers as she clenches around my length. I draw back leisurely, loving how tight and perfect she feels surrounding my cock. Her name falls from my lips like a prayer, "Be—

My fingers pause mid word, the hair on the back of my neck standing on end, I yank off my headphones and spin in my chair, gaze landing on Belle.

Holy fucking shit.

I whirl back around and slam my laptop closed, then snatch it off my desk, holding it securely over my boner. "How long have you been standing there?" I demand.

Her cheeks are pink as she licks her lips and attempts a nonchalant shrug. "Not long."

"And how long is that?"

She clears her throat. "A couple minutes, maybe…"

My eyes widen. She's standing close enough she would have been able to read over my—*Oh, fuck my life.* She *was* reading over my shoulder. The blush coating her cheeks and the way she's refusing to make eye contact says it all.

Belle waves a hand in the air, as if trying to clear the tension building between us. "It was like, two minutes, tops," she says when I silently stare at her for a full thirty seconds.

Now my heartrate is hammering through the roof for reasons other than the sex scene I was writing. She saw… Oh god, I was about to write *her* name. How do I get out of this without looking like a fucking psychopath?

"Val, take a breath," Belle coaches.

Christ, I didn't even realize I was holding it. I inhale deeply, making my head spin a little when I let it out in a woosh. "What are you doing here?"

She frowns. "You asked me to come look at your

laptop. Which by the way, seems to be working just fine."

Fuck. How could I have forgotten?

I clear my throat. "How'd you get in?"

She's still frowning. I don't like it, but there's nothing I can do about it.

"I knocked, and when you didn't answer, I let myself in with my key." She waves said key in my face.

"You're only supposed to use that to feed Muffin and Phyllis when I'm away, or in the highly unlikely case of an emergency."

"How was I to know you hadn't had a stroke died? I said I knocked. I even called out. Your car is in the drive, I knew you were home. I panicked."

I scoff. "Panicked? The unshakeable Hunter Sisters do not panic. Try again."

Belle throws her hands in the air and widens her eyes. "Fine! I saw you typing through the front window, and you never let me see this secret squirrel project of yours. If you'd just show me what it is, I wouldn't have to resort to unsanctioned key usage."

Now that my boner has completely deflated, I place my laptop back on the table, then slowly stand and turn to face my best friend. I am so pissed. I grip my hips to keep my hands from shaking. "You're kidding me, right? You don't tell *me* everything, but I don't go sticking my nose in your business, do I. Its private. I'm allowed to keep some things to myself."

Hurt flashes in her blue eyes before she steels herself, firming her jaw and mimicking my stance. "Actually, I do tell you everything. I thought we had the kind of friendship where we didn't keep secrets from each other. Guess I was wrong."

"Oh please, you don't talk to me about any of the guys you date. In fact, I haven't even met any of them." This is not an argument I want to have and I'm not entirely sure how we got here.

"You don't want to know about my love life Val. And you never met anyone because they don't mean anything to me. So why would I introduce you to them?"

I shake my head and run my hands through my hair, lacing my fingers behind my neck. "I don't know Bee, but you've met all of my girlfriends."

"That's because you're a serial monogamist. Your relationships are serious, mine never are."

"You're nearly thirty, it might be time to start thinking about changing that," I say. The words are out of my mouth before I can stop them. *Shit. Too far, too far. Abort!* "Sorry, you don't have to date seriously if you don't want to. I shouldn't have said that. I know you're *a strong, independent woman who doesn't need a man to complete her,"* I repeat the line she's been feeding me for years.

Officially over the argument, I sigh and meet her eyes, only to be met with…wait, why is she smiling? I shift on my feet. "Can we just forget this afternoon ever happened? Let's just scrap it and start over."

She tilts her face. "I don't know Val, can we?"

My brows furrow. "I hope so."

A moment of silence passes between us, then she asks, "If I tell you about the guys I've been seeing, will you let me read what you're working on?"

"No." This is the one and only thing I won't back down on. Belle can never read that manuscript. Ever. "You can ask me for anything else Bee, but not that."

Licking my lips, I move closer to her, taking one of her balled fists and holding it between my palms. "I'm not keeping secrets from you. It's just a story I've been playing with for a while and it's never going to see the light of day. I'm not keeping it *from* you Belle, I'm keeping *for* me."

Her fingers unfurl in my hold, and she nods slowly. "Fine."

I release her hand as I swiftly change the subject. "Give me a minute and I'll show you what I was talking about with my laptop. It's not the word processor that's giving me problems. When I go online, it lags and takes forever to load anything. Especially when I'm gaming."

"Alright, I'm just going to get myself a drink. You want one?" she asks, backing toward my kitchen.

"I'll have whatever you're having." I take a seat at the table and open my laptop. Quickly, I save then shut down the word document I'd been working on, then pull up my browser.

A few minutes later, Belle slides into the chair next to me and hands over a gin and tonic before reaching for the computer. I settle back with my drink as she taps away at the keyboard, opening and closing tabs and code boxes that mean absolutely nothing to me.

THAT *NEARLY THIRTY* COMMENT WAS THE MOMENT I decided that whatever he's hiding, I'm going to get to the bottom of it. Then he threw in *I'm not hiding it from you, I'm keeping it for me,* and I knew—I just knew—he was full of shit. Val and I don't keep things from each other. Period.

I'll stake out his house like a crazy ex-girlfriend if I have to. He was trying *way* too hard to keep me in the dark for whatever this secret of his is to be aboveboard. It's my job as his best friend to ensure he's not getting himself in to anything problematic.

With that settled in my mind, I smiled at him as he ranted about privacy and not needing to share everything with me and blah, blah, blah. I already had a plan in place.

Chapter Four

Belle

NEVER IN MY LIFE HAVE I HAD A PROBLEM SLEEPING. Never. But the last two nights, every time I close my eyes, I'm assaulted with visions of the scene Val was writing the other day. I swallow hard and sit up in my bed, scrubbing my hands over my face.

I hadn't meant to spy on him like that. I'd let myself in with the intent to sneak up and scare the crap out of him. And yes, when I noticed he was typing like a demon, I saw my chance, and I took it. But as my eyes caught on the words on the screen, that was it, I was done for. I couldn't look away as more and more words appeared, and they. Were. Hot.

He was clearly the hero of the story, seeing as the heroine moaned *his* name. *Why did I find that so sexy?*

I can see the whole thing in my mind, however it's not some mystery woman lying on the bedding beneath him, ass in the air, it's me... And god, do I want it. I've wanted it for years.

But I can't.

My throat aches as emotions I thought I'd buried build inside me, a tear slipping passed my iron clad will to hold them back. I haven't felt this alone in so long.

Throwing back the covers, I reach for the robe on the wingback chair beside my bed and slip my arms inside. I hate feeling sorry for myself, so I stride to my shoe closet, flicking on the lights as I enter. I flop down on the ottoman in the center of the room, admiring my collection. My pretties shine and sparkle all around me, and I smile.

FAINT STRAINS OF THE MELODY TO WHISKEY MYERS Stone penetrate my subconscious and my eyes pop open as I pitch upright. My arms flail in the air as my body slips to the side and I shriek before hitting the ground.

Flat on my back, I stare at the ceiling of my shoe closet. My gaze flicks from left, to right, as I try to figure out how I got in here. And then I remember... Damn Val and the saucy things I read over his shoulder. It's his fault I haven't been able to sleep the last couple of nights. His deliciously erotic words getting me all hot and bothered when I should be clocking a solid ten hours of shut eye.

My shoes always cheer me up when I'm feeling melancholy. However, I didn't plan on falling asleep on the ottoman last night. And I *definitely* didn't plan on having the hottest dream of my life either.

The chorus of Stone fills my ears, I sigh, then roll to my feet and trudge into my room to turn off my alarm before hitting the shower.

I'm beginning to second guess my plan to hack Val's laptop this weekend. If I find more of his super smut, I'll be ruined for any other man. But if I don't... I'll never stop wondering what he was trying so hard to hide.

WHEN I ARRIVE AT THE OFFICE I FEEL LIKE A ZOMBIE. I head straight for the breakroom and the box of glazed doughnuts in the middle of the table.

I'm halfway through my second when Ariel drops down on the couch beside me. I twist my head to look at her as I take another bite.

"You doin' okay?" she asks.

"Fine," I reply through a mouthful of sugary heaven.

Ariel cringes. "Two things. That's disgusting, and you are not fine. What's going on?"

"She's just realized she's in love with our honorary brother," Snow announces from the doorway.

Not true, I've always has a bit of a thing for Val, so the term brother makes me cringe. I lift my free hand to flip her off as I take another bite of my pastry. Giving Ariel my full attention, I ask, "What makes you think something's wrong?"

Her green eyes flit between Snow and I a couple of times before she says, "Your outfit is completely monotone, no color at all." She picks at the sleeve of my sheer slate-grey chiffon blouse. Then points down. "And what is on your feet? Are those, *flats*? I didn't even know you owned flats."

I shrug. "They're comfortable."

Her wide-eyed gaze flicks up to Snow. "911 responds to psychotic breaks, right?"

Snow chuckles. "She is taking all this harder than I expected. But I'd hold off on sending her to the loony bin just yet."

"Who's going to the loony bin?" Meg's voice comes from behind Snow a second before she pushes passed her to enter the room. I feel her gaze rake over me. "What the hell happened to her?"

I scoff. "Nothing *happened* to me. I'm just tired, I haven't been sleeping well. I'll be fine."

Meg arches a brow, Snow smirks, and Ariel narrows her eyes and murmurs beneath her breath, "She's wearing flats..."

Pushing up to my feet, I meet each of their gazes one at a time. "I'm fine. And they're not flats, they're kitten heels."

Ariel's face screws up in confusion then she leans to the side, staring at my shoes. "Since when do you wear anything with less than three inches?"

Done with the conversation, I shove the last bite of my doughnut in my mouth then get the hell away from my far too observant sisters. I was too drained to put any effort into my wardrobe this morning. Which is really saying something.

Clothes are my armor, my shield against the world. And I couldn't even be bothered suiting up. I don't look like a cat lady or anything, but my usual flair is missing. I throw myself into my work—which everyone knows better than to interrupt me from—for the rest of the morning.

By mid afternoon I've powered through everything I needed to do today, and I've successfully avoided speaking to anyone. But now I'm dying for a caffeine hit. I drag myself out of my chair and make my way to the breakroom to fix a cup of coffee only to hear my name from inside before I enter.

"Fifty says Belle will stop fighting it and throw herself at him by the end of next week. This has been a long time coming," Snow says.

My mouth pops open, those bitches are betting on me. Before I can bust in there and kick their asses, a much deeper voice than my sisters speaks up.

"Nah, she's too stubborn. Give it month," Kline says.

No freakin' way, I can't believe he's in on it too.

This is ridiculous.

My hands curl into fists and I take a step forward only to stop dead in my tracks when my dad's voice reaches my ears.

"Betting on my daughters would be bad parenting, so I'm not throwing any money in the ring. *But...* purely for hypothetical purposes, you understand, I'd—"

Oh hell no!

I storm into the room, fire blazing in my gaze as I attempt to scorch them all to ashes with my glare alone. "What is wrong with you people?"

Dad's eyes widen and he clears his throat. "Oh, hey princess."

"Don't you *princess* me," I snap. "Were you seriously getting in on this?"

He shrugs and slides his big hands into the pockets of his worn jeans. "I feel like I should say no, but that would be a lie..."

I shake my head. "You lot are worse than Edie Belesky and her pack of gossiping old women."

Dad looks appropriately chastened, but Snow, Kline, Ariel, and Meg, are clearly unrepentant if their bored expressions are anything to go by. And then I spot Doc, sitting on the couch, arms spread wide along the back, a cheery smile on his face.

"Oh come on! You too?" I ask.

Valentine's dad grins back at me. "I thought you two would have given me grandbabies by now. You're getting closer to your thirties every day. Me and your dad were shacked up and finished with the baby makin' by your age."

I snort. "And look how well that worked out for both of you."

Doc arches a brow. "Got something you wanna say little girl?"

"Val and Christian have different moms, and you're with a different woman every other week. No offence but you don't exactly scream *happy* to me." Now would be a good time for me to stop talking. But I've never been good at that, especially when I'm tired and stressed.

"And Dad's been miserable for the last twenty years. I'll pass on the devastating heartbreak thank you very much. Val and I are friends, he doesn't see me like *that*, so you lot need to get that through your heads." Before anyone can reply, I stalk from the room. Snatching my purse from the draw at my desk, I pause only to shut down my computers before I stride outside into the warm sunny day.

I'M SPRAWLED ON MY COUCH EATING ICE-CREAM FROM the carton and watching old episodes of The Nanny when my doorbell chimes.

I'm not in the mood for people, so I ignore it as Fran struts across my big screen T.V. in an ensemble I would kill for. Whoever is outside doesn't take the hint and begins banging on the door and repeatedly ringing the bell.

Glancing down at my sweats I groan. I am not fit for company. Val is the one and only person to seen me wear these. They may be designer, but they're still sweats, and I have a reputation to uphold.

"Go away," I call out.

"If you don't let me in princess, I'll let myself in," my dad's muffled voice responds through the closed door.

"I'm indecent," I return, pausing my show.

He's silent a beat, then calls back, "I'll close my eyes."

If a dad can't see his daughter at her worst, who can? I sigh and get up to let him in. When I swing the door open, his hand is covering his eyes. "It's fine, you can look," I tell him, returning to the couch and my tub of espresso ice-cream.

I hear him close the front door then his heavy footfalls approach the living room. He steps into view and takes a seat on one of the armchairs across from me, leaning his elbows on his knees as he sizes me up.

"Spit it out," I say, fully aware this is about my mini tantrum this afternoon.

His eyes intent on me, he starts, "I—" but then he pauses, dropping his gaze to the rug beneath the coffee table. "I'm sorry I didn't handle things better when your mom passed." His normally strong voice is ragged and thick with emotion.

A lump instantly forms in my throat, I wasn't expecting him to go there. He doesn't talk about that time. Ever.

He clears his throat, keeping his gaze averted. "You were right this afternoon when you called it devastating heartbreak. That's exactly what happened to me. I should have kept it together better though, for you girls. I should have shielded you from it. But I didn't and I'm sorry Belle."

When he lifts his eyes to mine, it's a struggle to swallow. I shake my head. "Daddy no. You did good. Really, you have nothing to be sorry for."

"Yes, I do. See, me falling apart made you girls see love as a bad thing. And that's the farthest thing from the truth. It was loving your mom that saved me in the first place. She gave me something worth living for, not just in her, but in you girls." He licks his lips and clasps his hands together between his spread knees.

Then he smiles, a true and genuine smile. The one he gets when he's thinking about her. "She was the best thing that ever happened to me. Then she gave me five more bests. I'm a lucky son of a bitch to have had her in my life for as long as I did. I don't regret a minute of time I spent with her, because she loved me as fiercely as I loved her."

"I know I was only a girl when we lost her, but I saw it. The love. I saw the devastation too. But you did nothing wrong; you were grieving. I don't fault you for it. None of us do. I don't think I would be able to handle it as well as you did." I swallow again, my throat aching from the intensity of my emotions.

Dad shakes his head, a sad smile tipping his lips, and sympathy shining in his blue eyes. "We don't know what we can handle until we have to princess. And I'm mad with myself for not noticing how much I screwed up you girls perception of love and its importance in life."

"You didn't—"

"I did. And I'm trying to make up for it now. You are in love with Valentine, Belle. You have been since you were a little girl. Your mom used to joke about the day you'd end up dragging that boy down the aisle. But he's just as mad about you, so I don't think there'll be too much dragging going on." He chuckles at his own joke while I gape at him.

"I don't remember her saying anything like that," I argue.

He snorts. "That's because you were off teaching Val how to play your video games, too busy to pay us any mind. I know he's your best friend. But it's okay for him to be more than that too."

I shake my head. "I already told you Val doesn't see me like that."

"You're so smart Belle, the smartest person I know, but you have some hairbrained ideas."

"What's that supposed to mean?" I demand.

He puts on a feminine voice as he repeats my words back to me, "Val doesn't see me like that." He chuckles and shakes his head.

I arch a brow, unimpressed with his attempt at humor. "He doesn't."

He rolls his eyes. "Yeah, okay princess."

"He doesn't," I insist, throwing my hands up.

"Let's agree to disagree on that, but it doesn't change the fact that you love him," he says, sitting back and crossing his arms over his chest, a smug smirk on his face.

I narrow my eyes. "I don't love him. I just... I don't know. It's complicated."

"Only because you're making it that way. I'm telling you right now he's mad about you, but you're too caught up in that big brain of yours to see it. Have you ever tried talking to him about your feelings?"

My nose wrinkles. "Eww, no. That would make

things weird between us. I mean, that's if I did have these supposed feelings."

Dad's brows furrow as he frowns at me. "That's it? That's what your worried about? What if he feels the same way? Did you ever consider that?"

I shove a spoonful of ice cream in my mouth and shrug.

"Belle," he says, tone serious.

"Yeah," I mumble mouth still full.

"What are you so afraid of?"

I swallow the ice cream. "You're asking what if he returns these hypothetical feelings. But what if he doesn't? Hmm, what then dad? Why ruin our friendship for nothing."

With a heavy sigh, he sits forward, elbows on his knees again. He levels me with a serious stare. "You girls are always betting on this and that, so now it's my turn. I bet you Valentine Foster is madly in love with you. If I'm wrong—which I'm not, because I never am, as you well know—I'll give you a hundred dollars."

I snort. "My best friend is worth more than a measly hundred."

"Fine, a grand."

"Pass," I tell him then shove another spoonful of ice cream in my mouth.

His shoulders slump. "All right then, you name the terms. Whatever you want."

An evil grin curves my lips as a diabolical idea pops into my head. There's no way he'll go for it. "You're on. When you lose—which you most definitely will—you have to go on a date. A real one. With a woman of my choosing."

His jaw tenses as he glares at me. But after a beat, he relaxes and shrugs his broad shoulders. "You have a deal."

Well, shit. That didn't go to plan...

Chapter Five

Valentine

Belle hasn't been herself all week, and she's been weird around me since our argument on Monday. I want to fix things, but I have no idea how to do that without giving up my secret guilty pleasure. I'm strumming my fingers against my desk, wracking my brain for an answer when Kida strolls in, with a big white bakery box in her arms.

She smiling as she approaches me, Bosco hot on her heels. "Hey Val! Want to sample my goodies?"

I choke back a laugh at the unexpected question.

I need to get my mind out of the gutter. "Umm, sure," I say when she opens the box and offers it to me.

"I've only been at it for a week, but Miss Gertie says I'm a natural," Kida tells me, pride radiating from her as she flicks one of her long blonde braids over her shoulder.

She's got the sweetest tooth of the girls, so I'm not at all surprised she's nailing it already. "That's awesome Keeds, I'm happy for you."

"Thanks Val," she murmurs, smiling so hard a dimple pops in her cheek.

Examining her offerings, I pick out a chocolate iced cupcake then glance up at her as I take a huge bite. The icing melts on my tongue and I grin as I chew. "Oh, my god Keeds, Miss Gertie wasn't wrong. This is delicious."

Her eyes shine with delight, her excitement contagious as she does a victorious fist pump. "You-wanna-know-something-cool? I'm going to tell you anyway. Cake legit makes you happy. There are studies out now that prove cake increases your happy hormones!"

"*Whore*moans," Kline sniggers as he walks passed.

I eye him. He's so fucking weird.

Kida snorts out a laugh and closes her *goodie box*. "I'm going to see who else wants to eat my treats."

"Okay, I'll catch you later." I reach down and give Bosco a scratch behind the ears, and he leans into my hand. I've missed the big lug hanging around here every day. He settles at my feet but keeps his eyes on Kida as she makes her way around to everyone in the pit. I rub his back with my foot until he gets up to follow her when she steps out of his line of sight into Miller's office.

The rest of the afternoon drags and I'm about to just get up and ask Belle outright if we're good when my cell chimes with a text. My eyes widen when my ex-girlfriend Maggie's name flashes across the screen. We haven't spoken since she tried to make me choose between my relationship with her and my friendship with Belle. That was over five months ago, I didn't expect to hear from her again.

MAGGIE: Hey Val, can we meet up for a coffee? I feel really bad about the way things ended between us and I need to apologize.

I stare at the text. She wants to apologize? That's, that's...wow.

Belle

AFTER COMING TO TERMS WITH THE BET I STUPIDLY made with Dad the other day I've been trying to work out how to approach Val. I could let him in on the stakes of the bet without telling him what the actual bet is…

No. I scrap that idea before it even fully forms. Hunters don't cheat.

I need to win this bet. Dad hasn't been on a date in forever. He's tried a couple of times over the years, a date here and there, but nothings ever come of it. We all hate seeing him alone. I'm not naive enough to think he doesn't have sex, but he deserves to have someone to share his life with.

If I lost though… That would mean I'd have Val. Like, really have him. He'd be mine. My pulse picks up at the notion of Val being more than my best friend.

But I'm not stupid enough to think I've just missed the cues all this time. I mean, not once in all the years we've been friends has he tried to put the moves on me. Not even when I'm drinking, and my inhibitions take a vacay.

No, Val doesn't see me that way, and I'm kinda scared that telling him about my secret crush will change our dynamic. I don't want to make things weird and awkward between us.

Our friendship has always been easy and natural. We just work together. As friends. I don't even know if we would work well as lovers. My fantasies say hells yes, we'd be fire. But my brain says, what if we're not? What if, by some unlikely miracle, he reciprocates my feelings, and we try being more and we're not compatible?

I'd lose him. My stomach churns at the thought and I regret eating that slice of cheesecake Kida gave me. Even if it was smooth and creamy and disgustingly delicious. I hate feeling this way. The uncertainty makes me nauseous.

Closing my eyes, I realign my thoughts. I consciously push away all the negativity swirling through my head. Telling Valentine how I feel will *not* end our friendship. No matter what happens, we'll always have that. Even if things get uncomfortable between us for a bit, over time it would get better. I'm sure of it.

I live by the motto that Cinderella is proof that a

new pair of shoes can change your life. So, with that in mind, I click over to my favorite shopping site, and pick out a gorgeous little pair of pale pink GIANVITO ROSSI Alisia Mules. Two minutes later my purchase is complete and I'm ready for whatever comes next.

Standing from my desk, I smooth my hands down my grey knit skirt, then stride across the pit to face Val. He's slumped in his chair with one arm hooked over the back of it as he stares at his cell. He's frowning at the screen and my brows dip as draw closer. I nibble my bottom lip as I decide whether to interrupt him or not.

Before I've made up my mind, he lifts his head, and his eyes meet mine. "Hey, I was just about to come over to see you," he says.

My frown deepens. "You were? What for?"

"I actually don't remember now," he chuckles, but there's an awkward edge to it.

"Is everything okay?" I ask, eyeing his cell.

He glances at it and shrugs. "I think so. Maggie texted."

I scowl. I hate that chick. "What's she want?"

Val's expression turns pensive. "To see me."

My face screws up in distaste. What could she possibly want now? If she thinks I'll just stand back and let her hurt him again, she's got another think coming.

"Whoa there, killer, calm down. She says she wants to apologize," he says.

I fold my arms and pop a hip. "As she should. But she can do that via text. There's no reason she needs to do it in person."

He chuckles. "True."

"So, what are you going to do?"

He shrugs. "I don't know. I mean, I don't want to be a dick. If she wants to apologize, I can give her that."

"You're too nice for your own good, you know that."

"Nah, I just don't see the point in lowering myself to other people's level. It won't hurt me any to meet her for a coffee so she can say whatever she needs to, and then she can move on."

I arch a brow. "Like I said, too nice."

Val chuckles and shakes his head at me. "Anyway, what brings you to my side of the pit?"

"Umm..." I was going to ask him to come over tonight, get him nice and drunk, spill my guts, wait for his inevitable rejection, then move on to planning Dad's date. But with Maggie reappearing I don't think now is the best time for me to throw a spanner in me and Val's friendship.

I mean yeah, the whole purpose of getting him drunk before I tell him is so he'll hopefully not remember any of it the next day. But on the off chance he does recall me dropping this bomb on him, he'll probably need a bit of space afterward.

Shit, shit, shit.

"Umm, Bee…" Val says. "Are you all right?"

"Me? Yeah, of course. I'm fine. I umm, I forgot what I was going to say, too. Can't have been that important, then." I back away from him. "I'll let you know if I remember." Then I powerwalk back to my corner of the pit, collapse into my chair, and rub my temples.

My head hurts, my heart hurts, and my stomach is in knots.

Snow sidles up to me and I side eye her. "What do you want?"

She hooks her thumb over her shoulder. "I saw that little exchange. You okay? You look like shit when you're stressed."

"Thanks," I deadpan.

"What? Would you prefer I lie to you?"

I sigh. "Not now, Snow; I'm not in the mood. So, unless you need something, leave me alone."

"Nah, I'm good; was just seeing if you were," she says with a shrug.

"I'm fine."

She arches a brow. "You're not, but whatever. You don't have to tell me about it if you don't want to. I probably wouldn't have anything constructive to say, anyway." With that, she strides away, leaving me to my brewing headache.

BY THE TIME LUNCH ROLLS AROUND I'M DYING TO GET some fresh air and some much needed space. I grab my purse and walk the few blocks to Main Street. I arrive at Perky's Books & Brews on the tail end of the lunch rush so there's only a couple of people ahead of me as I line up to order.

While I'm waiting, I browse this week's *He's a ten, but...* display. I've read a few of them already and pick up the first new-to-me title I see. The Post-it on this one says, *He's a ten, but... He's her son's best friend and it's not what you think*. I scan the blurb and it sounds like a good read, so I pick up a copy to buy then return the labeled one to the top of the stack.

Turning back to the counter my jaw hardens. Maggie stands in front of me, a self-righteous smile on her annoyingly pretty face.

"Belle, hey! I was hoping I'd see you soon," she says.

I stare at her; she's rocking a new look. Her hair is lighter, and her outfit is on point. If I didn't hate her, I'd probably like it. I deliberately keep my face expressionless as I ask, "And why is that?"

"Can we sit? I need to talk to you."

Umm, no. "Yeah, no. I don't have a lot of time."

She places a hand on my forearm. "It won't take long."

I scowl and step away from her touch, but then my guardian angel Perky, calls out, "You're up Belle; what'll it be, sweetie?"

I shoot Miss Perky an appreciative chin lift, then excuse myself from Maggie's conniving ass even as she smiles pleadingly at me. It's fake as shit because Maggie is fake as shit. "I really don't have the time right now. Maybe another day."

Or maybe never.

"Okay, it's just, with Valentine and I getting back together, I really wanted to clear the air between us," she says.

And my stomach drops. I pivot to face her. "Excuse me?"

Maggie frowns. "Oh, he didn't tell you?"

"That would be a negative, Maggie. Seeing as how Val doesn't want anything to do with you."

Her smile turns malicious. "You poor love, you're misinformed. Sounds like you and Valentine aren't as close as you think."

Folding my arms and tucking my book against

my side I glare at her. "Then maybe you should enlighten me."

"We're going out tomorrow. That's not exactly the behavior of someone who doesn't want anything to do with me. Wouldn't you say?"

This chick. She's starting to make me stabby. "Look Maggie, Val's too nice to say it, so allow me to do it for him. Stay. The. Fuck. Away." I take a step closer to her with each pointed word. When I'm mere inches from her, I lower my chin and stare her down.

The corner of her mouth kicks up in a smirk. An actual freaking smirk. Violence thrums in my veins. If it wasn't for my impeccable nails, I'd punch her in her smug face. She hurt Val so badly when she offered up her ultimatum. What kind of person does that? And now she thinks she can just waltz back into his life.

Over my dead body.

Maggie tilts her face to the side, and that's when I catch a flash of crazy eyes. Well shit. If I was a betting woman, which I am, I'd say Maggie is about to become a problem.

WHEN STAKING OUT YOUR BFF'S HOME, IT'S WISE TO have a solid excuse ready to go should you be discovered. And lucky for me, Maggie just made herself the perfect scape goat.

It's two in the morning, Val should be well and truly into REM as I stride up his driveway like it's perfectly normal for me to be here at this hour. It's all about confidence. I can't have the neighbors reporting a suspicious lurker to the cops.

Once I reach the front stoop, I sidestep, spin, then drop into a squat behind the shrubs that line the front wall. With my back pressed to the scratchy brick surface I crabwalk sideways until I'm positioned close to his computer desk.

Retrieving a picnic blanket from my huge purse, I spread it out, then drop to my ass on it before pulling out my laptop. Then I get to work.

It takes seconds to login to his WIFI network, allowing me to effortlessly hack his server. I skip over all the boring stuff like bank records and tax receipts. When I find what I think I'm looking for, I cringe.

Oh, Val. It's not even in an encrypted file—no password protections, nothing. I really need to talk to him about device security.

With a couple of taps on my trackpad, I find a single folder full of word docs. I quickly count them, five. Given their sizes, they're not small documents. Each of them ranges from two to four hundred kilobytes. I click on the one that was most recently accessed and start reading.

I keep reading.

And reading.

And reading.

Chapter Six

Valentine

STEPPING OUT THE FRONT DOOR, I'M STILL NOT SURE how I feel about meeting up with Maggie this morning. I can't for the life of me figure out why she suddenly wants to apologize. She was furious when I refused to choose between my girlfriend and my best friend. But being the nice guy I am, I agreed to meet her for a coffee at Perky's.

I'm locking the front door when something pink catches my eye. I turn my head to the left and just about fall off the stoop at the sight of Belle sleeping behind my hedge. I creep over and poke her shoulder. "Bee, what are you doing?"

She jolts awake, a confused look on her face and a few twigs in her hair. She glances around at our surroundings, and mutters, "Shit."

I have so many questions. "Ah, want to tell me why you're sleeping in my shrubs?"

"Umm... I ah..." She runs a hand through her hair, her fingers snagging on a knot. She clears her throat as she removes a twig. "Well, okay, so I ran into Maggie yesterday afternoon, and she gave off some seriously f'ed up vibes, Val. I was worried she might show up here and cause a scene or something. I was just keeping an eye out."

I arch a brow. "From the shrubbery?"

"That's how stakeouts work. I wasn't going to sit out in the open."

I nod, as technically that's correct. "Right yeah, I know that. But," I gesture at her disheveled appearance. "What the fuck, Bee?" Her appearance is probably the most concerning part of all this. Belle is never anything but completely put together. Ever.

She sighs and shuffles around until she's leaning against the wall. "You know, a thank you would be nice. I slept on the ground for you, Valentine. You could at least show a little appreciation."

This is weird, even for us. But I don't have time

to get into it right now. "You want a hand up?" I extend my arm to her.

With a roll of her eyes, she places her palm in mine and allows me to help her stand. I pick up her blanket then reach for her discarded laptop.

"I got it!" she yelps, snatching it out of my reach just as my fingertips graze its edge. A brilliant smile stretches across her face as she deposits it in her massive purse, then takes the blanket from me and shoves it in, too. "Well, I better go. I'll see you later." Then she's jogging down my drive—in six inch heels —like this is a totally normal morning.

I STROLL IN TO PERKY'S JUST AFTER NINE AND SURVEY the filled tables. There's always quite a crowd here on Saturday's. I don't spot Maggie on my first sweep across the room, so I do another. She used to harp on about punctuality like she was paid to, so I know she's here somewhere.

On my second pass around the area, a blonde woman waves at me, and I do a double take before realizing its Maggie. When I reach her, she stands, wrapping her arms around me in a tight hug.

"I'm so glad you came!" she gushes.

Extricating myself, I hold her at arm's length.

"Hey, Mags." She beams at me, and I force a smile in return.

"I already ordered for us. I know what my man likes," she states with a coy smile, then lowers herself onto a loveseat and beckons me to join her.

With no other seating options, I reluctantly I drop down next to her, trying to leave a modicum of space between us. Unfortunately, I fail. This seat is too small for two people who used to be in a relationship. But the fact that she chose it tells me I'm not just here to hear this apology. That and the *my man* comment.

"You ah, changed your hair," I say lamely, gesturing to her new, longer, blonder locks.

"I did; do you like it?" She preens, toying with the ends of it.

I shrug. "It's all right." I'm a dude, I don't really care about hair.

Maggie's shoulders slump a little, but she quickly shakes it off and her smiles widens. Placing her hand on my thigh, she leans into my space. "You're probably wondering why I waited so long to reach out again."

"Not really. You made it pretty clear where you stood when you walked out on me," I tell her. I don't know what she thinks she's doing, but I'm not encouraging it.

Her smile faulters, but again, she rallies. "I was hurt and confused. I appreciate you giving me time and space to think things through. And I have, Valentine. I've thought long and hard about our relationship and I'm just not willing to give it all up for something as trivial as a little jealousy. I'm ready to forgive you and move forward."

My brows hike up my forehead. "Mags, *I* didn't do anything requiring forgiveness. You're the one who threw an epic bitch fit and stormed out of my house after calling me an array of names I'm not going to repeat. So, I'm not sure what you're talking about."

She bats my shoulder as she throws her head back and... *laughs.*

I eye her, worried she's about to pull some full blown sociopath shit right here in the middle of Perky's. Glancing around, she appears to have gained quite a bit of attention. I throw the other patrons what I hope is a reassuring smile, then turn back to my nutso ex-girlfriend.

"What's so funny, Mags?" I ask, half afraid of her answer. She wasn't crazy when we were dating last year. It wasn't until the last month or so when she started trying to gaslight me about my friendship with Belle. Then there was the ultimatum. But the way she's behaving is setting off all kinds of alarms in my head.

When her gaze returns to me, she takes my hand between hers, brings it to her lips, then brushes a kiss against my knuckles. "I always was the pursuer in our relationship, wasn't I?" She sighs wistfully, then lowers my hand to hold it in her lap.

As gently as possible, I disentangle my hand from her grip. "Ah, yeah. I guess so. But I fail to see what that has to do with anything."

She chuckles, leaning in and swiping a few strands of hair off my forehead. "You want me to apologize, I understand. And I am sorry, Valentine. I caused us both needless pain, and I deeply regret the months we've spent apart. But I'm here now, and we can pick up where we left off."

A waitress arrives, placing two mugs on the small coffee table before us. She shoots us a quick smile before moving on to deliver another order.

Once she's out of earshot, I shake my head, displacing Maggie's hand from where it's now cupping the side of my neck. "Pick up where we left off? What are you even talking about? We're done. And have been for the last six months. You made sure of that with your extremely offensive accusations. And you expect me to forget that?"

"Water under the bridge," she says, her eyes becoming glassy.

I squint, really looking into her eyes for the first time since I sat down. "Are you, are you wearing contacts?"

She perks up again. "Do you like them?"

Shifting as far back from her as I can without falling off this damn loveseat, I take a moment to catalogue her. She's changed more than her hair. She's wearing blue contacts, a full face of make-up, a form fitting navy dress, and heels Belle would probably kill for.

My eyes widen as it all comes together.

She's transformed herself into Belle. Or tried to.

Jesus. H. Christ. She *is* a sociopath. Or a psychopath. Either way, this is fucked.

"Well?" Maggie prompts.

I'm drawing a blank. What were we just talking about? "What was the question again?"

She grins and shoves me playfully. "My contacts, silly. Do you like them?"

"Oh, right. Umm, yeah, they're nice." This answer seems to unsettle her, yet please her at the same time. Her expression wars between the two emotions. I don't want to upset the crazy, so I rush to add, "But your eyes are pretty without them."

Mollified, she smiles coyly and tucks a strand of

hair behind her ear. "Thanks, Val, you always know just what to say."

I strongly disagree, but that's a moot point at this juncture in time. Maggie clearly has a few loose screws upstairs. I wish Meg were here, she'd know how to handle this situation. I probably should have listened better when she gave that presentation on talking down mentally unstable skippers.

I'm about to excuse myself with the lamest excuse ever—bathroom break—so I can call Meg when Belle walks in. Maggie stiffens at my side, and I'm instantly on high alert.

Belle doesn't notice us at first, or at least she pretends not to. As she draws closer to the counter her gaze swings our way, she smiles and gives us a little finger wave. Movement at her feet pulls my attention downwards, and I'm shocked to find Bosco at the end of a shiny black leather leash.

My brows dip, Belle's far from a fan of his so what's she doing with him? A quick survey of the store makes it clear Kida isn't with them. I stare at the duo in confusion, then notice Bosco isn't wearing his regular collar, but a fancy black number with a bowtie on it. I snort a laugh, trust Belle to dress up a dog.

"What's so funny?" Maggie asks, still stiff as a board.

"The dog, he's wearing a bowtie," I say, pointing at Bosco.

"Oh. Maybe we should ask her to join us? It looks like she's alone," Maggie suggests.

I swing my head to stare at her. I can't read her expression, but her posture is still rigid. "Nah, it's okay. She probably has plans."

"With who? Is she finally seeing someone?"

"I don't know, maybe."

"Why does she have that dog with her anyway? I thought she hated animals."

I shrug. "Not sure. And she doesn't hate anything, she just doesn't like it when Bosco uses her shoes for chew toys."

"Hmph," Maggie huffs, her artificial blue eyes focused on Belle. Then a smile tugs at her lips, and she turns her attention back to me. She places a hand high on my thigh and snuggles in close to my side. "I actually saw her in here yesterday. She was surprisingly supportive of you and I reconnecting. I told her I wanted to clear the air between us, but she wouldn't have it. Wasn't that sweet of her? She could have treated me terribly for the way I acted."

Well, that's a crock of shit if I ever heard one. "Really, she was?" I ask, playing along.

Maggie nods, a blinding smile lighting her face. "She's your best friend and she just wants you to be happy. I understand that now. I can't believe I was jealous of her before. I guess I was just insecure, but I won't let it come between us again. I promise." She gives my thigh a little squeeze and rests her cheek on my shoulder.

I have no idea what part of all that I should respond to first. I shift on the seat, but Maggie just snuggles in closer, wrapping her free hand around my bicep. I curl my fingers around her wrist, pry her hand off me, and get to my feet. "Look Mags, I'm glad you've made your peace with Belle. But we aren't getting back together."

She tilts her head to the side, her eyes boring into me. "What are you talking about? That's why you came here, so I could say sorry, and then we can move on, together."

"No, I came because you said you wanted to apologize. That's it. End of. And now, I'm leaving. Have a good life Mags; I hope you find happiness."

I swear her eye twitches as she launches to her feet. "Why am I not good enough for you anymore? You said you loved me. Was it all a lie?"

Oh, my fucking god. All eyes turn to us. Their curious stares make my skin itch. I hate being the center of attention. I grit my teeth and lean into her, keeping my voice low I growl, "Don't do that,

Maggie. You walked away from me, not the other way around."

"I wouldn't have had to if you put that little slut you call your best friend in her place. But no, you wanted it all. The faithful girlfriend and your *sidepiece*," she sneers, throwing a savage glare Belle's way.

My eyes widen. *Fuck me.* "What are you even talking about?"

"All right Miss Thang, you need to leave. Nobody disrespects my girls and gets to finish their coffee," Perky interjects, stepping in between Maggie and me.

Maggie sniffles. "Sure, blame the victim."

"Victim?" I bark. "Victim of what? You're delusional."

Literally everyone in the place is staring at us as Maggie wails then launches herself at me. Her fists pound against my chest and when I grab one of her wrists, she rakes the nails of her free hand down the side of my face.

"Fuck," I grumble.

Before I can snatch up her free hand, Belle appears behind Maggie. She seizes her flailing arm, twisting it up behind her back until Maggie yelps in pain. Then she takes the wrist I'm holding and draws it up to meet the other. She jabs the tip of her pointed heel into the back of Maggie's knees, dropping her to the ground where she forces her flat and straddles her back.

Maggie shrieks in outrage and thrashes uselessly in Belle's hold.

"Zip ties, in my bag," Belle says to me, gesturing with her chin toward her discarded purse.

I grab it and riffle through it. "You sure this isn't Mary Poppin's bag, how much shit do you need in here?" I grouse.

"You can never be too prepared," she says, not even the least bit put out by the still raging Maggie.

Passing the ties over, Belle swiftly secures her wrists then stands. She moves to my side, loops her arm through mine and meets Maggie's enraged glare with a smirk. "Oh honey, didn't I tell you yesterday? Val and I are together now. Turns out you were right; he and I are a perfect match."

Then she slides her fingers into my hair, turns my face to her, and crushes her mouth to mine.

Chapter Seven

Belle

HOLY SHIT, I'M KISSING VAL... OH, GOD, WHAT WAS I thinking! And why does it feel so freaking good?

Val takes over the kiss before I can end it. One of his big palms lands on the small of my back, drawing me in closer to his body as he tips my chin up with his free hand, changing the angle of our kiss. His tongue glides over my bottom lip and I sigh happily.

Maggie's furious shriek pierces my ears.

Oh, yeah, that's what started all this.

Reluctantly, I sever our connection and peer

down at her. "Just so you know, Val will be pressing charges." Then I retrieve my cell from my back pocket and put in a call to a friend of mine at the local PD.

Within twenty minutes Maggie is being escorted into the back of a squad car, and the onlookers at Perky's are being interviewed. Val hasn't said a word to me since I pried my lips from his. And if I hadn't read what I did last night, I'd think he was pissed at me for pulling that little stunt.

As he gives Officer Taylor his statement his posture is tense and every now and again, he throws me a weird look. I'm not sure if it's because he's trying to wrap his head around Maggie's cray-cray display or if he's just confused about what I did.

Honestly, I'm a little confused myself. I mean, I know I've been playing with the idea of fessing up about my feelings not being completely friendly, but I wasn't intending to lay one on him in the middle of Perky's. I had a plan, damn it, and this was not it. I gnaw on my bottom lip as I consider my next move.

Maybe I should leave to give him some space to work through his thoughts on his own. I know I sure as hell need to get my head on straight after that kiss, along with everything I read last night. I didn't even finish before I fell asleep. Which I'm pissed about doing. Who falls asleep on a secret mission? I was supposed to be out of there hours before Val woke up.

Come to think of it, I'm pretty sure I neglected to import the file before I started reading. Goddamn it. That means I'll have to go back again. Cause there is no way in hell I'm letting this slide, but I want to finish the damn manuscript before I broach the topic with him. It was so good. It sucked me in until I forgot I was sitting in his shrubs, in the middle of the night.

Scooping up my purse, I head for the door, only to pause when Perky calls, "Forgetting something, Missy?"

Shit. I spin on my heel and take the end of the black leather leash she holds out for me. "Thanks," I murmur, then lead Bosco out to the footpath. He trots along happily at my feet, his tongue hanging out the side of his mouth as he goes.

Ugh, so gross.

This morning when I got home, I found a note stuck to my front door, then discovered Bosco and his favorite squeaky pink pig on my back deck.

I wouldn't ask if I had another option. Arlo and I are going up to the city for the weekend and after what happened last time, Bosco isn't welcome for a little while. It's not his fault one of the girls fed him a whole block of

*cheese right before we left the house to go out to dinner
and he wasn't allowed to come with us to the fancy
schmancy restaurant, and while we were gone things got...
umm, messy.*

*But you won't feed him cheese, so there's nothing to worry
about! I promise he'll be a good boy and we'll pick him up
when we get back tomorrow night.*

Kisses, Kida

I'll have to have a word with Keeds about the difference between asking and doing a dump and run. She clearly has the two confused. Regardless, I'm stuck with the drool demon for the rest of the day and all of tomorrow.

I don't know why someone else couldn't take him. We have three other sisters plus dad. Hell, even Doc would have happily taken the slobber pot. Not to mention Val. He would have done it and been grateful for the time with the mutt.

When we get home, I hesitate at the front door. Bosco sits patiently at my feet, staring up at me. I glare back at him. "If you so much as look at my shoes, you're done. You understand me? I'll drop you at the pound and tell them I found you in an alley going through trash."

He blinks, then his tongue flops out and he pants. I take that as his assent, then open the door and release his leash. He waddles inside like he owns the place, his tiny little stump of a tail wiggling as he goes, and I have to admit... it's kind of cute. Especially when he heads straight to the bed—okay, mini-throne—I got for him from a cute little pet boutique online. Who knew you could get such cute stuff for dogs?

I DON'T HEAR FROM VAL FOR THE REST OF THE DAY and I'm kinda freaking out about it. I mean... I kissed him, for god's sake.

My head spins and I drop down on the edge of the couch and grip my temples. What was I thinking? It was that damn story I started reading last night. It put ideas in my head. Ideas like Val might actually share my feelings but hasn't said anything up to this point for the same reasons as me.

Yeah, he kissed me back this morning, but maybe he only did that to keep from embarrassing me. Or to get the message through to Maggie that they were done.

I'm pretty sure that's why I did it in the first place, I'm a little fuzzy on the details after she laid her hands on him. I saw red, and everything that happened next is a bit of a blur until my lips brushed against his and it all came roaring back into focus.

Prior to last night, kissing Val to prove a point wouldn't have even manifested itself as an option to me. And look at me now... sitting alone in my house having a minor panic attack because I'm pretty sure I've fucked everything up.

I remind myself to breathe through the anxiety flooding my system. A warm weight settles against my calf. Bosco peers up at me, concern in his big brown eyes. Kida originally got him as a companion dog for when she had bouts of anxiety. I've seen him do this exact thing to Keeds a hundred times, yet I never put it together. He's comforting and grounding her, just like he's doing for me now.

"Thanks, big guy," I murmur, reaching down to scratch behind his ear. He leans into my touch, and for the first time ever, I feel a connection to him, like he's more than just a shoe destroying lump of drool.

And then, he farts, ruining the moment and triggering my gag reflex as the rancid odor permeates my entire living room.

"Oh, god!" I launch off the couch, sprinting for the front door. I throw it open, burst out into the night and drop to my knees as I gasp for fresh air. The dirty little bastard trots out after me and plops his fat ass on the grass at my side, his long tongue lolling to the side as he smiles up at me.

I glare at him, and if looks could kill, he'd be in puppy purgatory.

Valentine

IT'S BEEN ELEVEN HOURS AND THIRTY-EIGHT MINUTES since Belle kissed me.

I can't stop thinking about it. Over and over, it replays in my mind. Her lips... those incredible lips that I've dreamed about a million times... finally sweeping across mine. I was stunned at first, taken totally off guard. But it took less than two seconds for my brain to get on board, and I pulled her close and went for it.

And then Maggie screamed her freakin' lungs out and shattered the moment.

Fucking Maggie.

Pacing back and forth across my living room for the umpteenth time since I got home, I run my hands through my hair. I've been trying to figure out what I should do, if anything, and what she was thinking.

Was it just about Maggie? Was that her motivation? Or was it something more? Like, had she been thinking about kissing me and saw it as the perfect opportunity to finally lay one on me?

I close my eyes and shake my head.

Get a grip, man.

I'm still pacing when a crash sounds from the side of the house. Peering out the window, I don't see anything, so I head out to have a look. When I round corner to my trash cans I'm met with the most adorably huge dark eyes.

"Hey, there, little guy," I croon to the juvenile racoon raiding my garbage. He's frozen in place, his little paws clutching a banana peel. He's so freakin cute. I move toward him slowly, then crouch down a few feet from him.

His head tilts to the side as he watches me carefully. I do a quick survey of the mess he's made and spot a scrap of an old dinner roll. I reach out and grab it, then offer it to him. He eyes the roll, then me, then the roll again.

"It's okay, I won't hurt you. Take it," I encourage.

After a full minute, he shuffles closer, then snatches it from my fingertips and scurries back again. This time all the way to the edge of the garden bed. I smile and give him a wave; sure he'll be back soon.

"Night, buddy," I call after him as he disappears into the darkness.

It's not the first time I've seen him. He's been hanging around for the last few weeks and I'd be lying if I said I didn't like it. How anyone could hate trash pandas is beyond me. They're the cutest fucking things around. And I'm honored he keeps coming back to my trash. Although, I think I'll just start leaving out some scraps for him, so he doesn't need to make such a mess.

By the time I'm done tidying up after him, I'm tired and ready to call it a night. I have a quick shower, then crawl into bed, more than ready for a reprieve from my thoughts. Unfortunately, that doesn't quite happen.

I dream of our kiss. Of Belle throwing down for me, then claiming me as hers in front of half the town. Only difference is, it doesn't stop there. In my dreams we leave Perky's together, and for the first time in the history of our long friendship, I make love to my best friend.

By the time Monday rolls around, Belle and I still haven't spoken. Mostly because I couldn't decide how to handle the kiss.

I'm so sexually frustrated, I added three more sex scenes to my current manuscript. It now has significantly more banging in it than anything I've previously written. I can't shake the feel of her perfect curves pressed against me and the soft brush of her full lips from my thoughts.

My knee bounces relentlessly as I sit waiting for the weekly meeting to start. Belle hasn't arrived yet. No surprises there; she's never been on time for anything in her life. Snow is leering at me from across the table, so I arch a brow at her. "Can I help you?"

She smirks. "How was your weekend?"

"Fine." I narrow my gaze. Snow isn't into small talk.

Her eyes practically sparkle as she shares a look with Ariel, who is sitting beside her. Those two have some weird telepathic connection and it creeps me out.

With a smug grin, Ariel says, "We heard there was some excitement down at Perky's Saturday morning."

"Yeah, Maggie lost her shit," I tell them, hoping it's enough and that it's all they're referring to.

"Uh-huh, sounds titillating. But that's not what we're interested in," Snow says.

I swallow. Figures the town gossip mill would focus on the kiss and not the psycho who attacked me. Still, I feign ignorance. "You mean Belle kicking her ass? Yeah, that was pretty fucking spectacular."

Snow scowls, and Ariel rolls her eyes, just as Meg drags the chair out beside her.

"What are we talking about?" Meg asks, her gaze bouncing between the three of us.

"Val and Belle kissed over the weekend," Snow announces.

Before I can shush her, my dad bellows, "About fucking time."

My head snaps in his direction. "Excuse me?"

He ignores me and turns his attention to Snow. "Did anyone have money on the weekend?"

She grins triumphantly. "Me. Pay up, losers."

"Are you serious?" I demand.

Her signature smirk tips her blood red lips. "Deadly."

I shake my head, what else can I do. These girls and their freakin' bets. And how the hell did my dad get involved? On second thought, I don't want to know.

"So, when are you two moving in? I'm assuming

soon seeing as it's taken so damn long for you to finally get your shit together," Dad says.

I choke on air then glare at him. "One kiss doesn't change anything. We're not a thing. She kissed me to drive the point home to Maggie that we were done. That's it."

A choir of groans fill the room, and I gape at them all.

"What? If I've told you once, I've told you a thousand times, Belle isn't into me. She's my bes—"

"Best friend, yeah, we know. We've heard it all before, from both of you and we're all sick of watching you two circle each other like a pair of lovesick fools. It's time to shit or get off the pot. You need to get your head out of your ass, son. Make a damn move on your girl, already," Dad says, his gaze as serious as I've ever seen it.

I swallow hard, taken aback by his stern demeanor. My old man is a happy go lucky, live life by the seat of your pants kind of guy. He doesn't do stern or serious. I open my mouth to respond, then slam it closed again as Belle strides into the room in a flouncy black mini skirt, a snug white button up blouse with a black bowtie and a sunshine yellow blazer. She heads straight for me, taking the chair beside mine.

Snow smirks and I shoot her a glare, shaking my

head. Thankfully, she heeds my warning and remains silent on the matter, as does everyone else. That doesn't stop my pulse from shooting through the roof at Belle's nearness, though.

My dad's words scroll through my head on a loop. They've heard it all before, from both of us. What does that mean? Have they had this same conversation with Belle? And if so, does that mean she really does want me, but thinks I don't want her?

What a clusterfuck this is all turning out to be. And I can't keep doing it. I need to know once and for all if there's a chance for us. But first, I need to pay attention to what Miller is saying at the head of the table. Afterwards though… Afterwards I'm doing what I should have done years ago.

I close my eyes and take a breath, but it backfires.

I'm assaulted by her sweet honey and vanilla fragrance and Jesus Christ, why me? I grit my teeth and try like hell to ignore how alluring I find every damn thing about her, especially her signature scent.

"Morning, Val," she murmurs, leaning into my space.

"Hey," I mumble, trying like hell to concentrate on anything but her.

Her brows furrow. "You okay?"

I give her a tight nod. "Yep. Great."

Fuck, fuck, fuck.

I have no idea how to handle this. I've wanted her for so long. Now, knowing it's a possibility is driving me insane. My dick is already chubbing up just thinking about it.

One part of my brain is telling me to be cool. Act like her kissing me was a totally normal thing to do and play it off. The other, *hornier,* part says fuck that, drag her ass out of here and do what needs to be done. I groan and drop my face into my hands.

Belle's palm comes to rest on the back of my neck, her nails gently scratching up into the hair at the base of my skull. I lift my head to meet her gaze.

Christ, she's beautiful.

If she'd just give me a sign, nothing could stop me from making her mine. And then she shifts almost nervously and begins strumming her nails against the tabletop and as I reach for her hand to still it, something that's never happened before transpires...

Chapter Eight

I DON'T THINK VAL HAS EVER LOOKED AT ME THE WAY he is right now and my stomach flutters as a million butterflies take flight.

This morning I woke up from yet another deliciously dirty dream starring Val and me. I'm far from rested, and extremely frustrated. A vibrator can only do so much. And the look in his eyes has lusty thoughts racing through my brain. I flush and drop my hand from his neck, turning to face dad at the head of the table as he hands a stack of cases to Ariel.

Work. I need to focus on work.

I do my best to keep my attention on what dad's saying, but it's not holding my interest. I already know what he's telling the others. I put those case files together for them. I strum my nails against the timber tabletop, too restless to be still.

Val places his hand over mine, giving my fingers a little squeeze, at contact an electric current zips up my arm. I shiver and slide my hand out from under his. That's never happened before. And even now, without the physical contact between us, a phantom echo of his touch remains, and the current continues to flow.

I glance at him from the corner of my eye. I need to know if he feels it too, this shift. He's stiff beside me, shoulders set, jaw tight, and his hands are balled into fists on his thighs. He swallows hard and my gaze fixes on his Adams apple as it bobs with the motion. I want to lick it… and other things.

My eyes shoot wide, and I quickly glance around at the others seated at the table. I feel like my lascivious thoughts are plastered all over my face. But nobody's paying me any mind, except that is, for Val.

Without warning, a screech fills the room as he

shoves back his chair, takes my hand then yanks me out of mine. He doesn't say a word as he strides to the door, tugging me along behind him. Not that I'm arguing.

With our fingers twined together he leads me to the other side of the building, stopping at... the storage closet? "Uh, Val?"

"Hmm..." he hums in response as he flips on the light, then locks the door behind us. He tests the handle before turning to face me with a gleam in his eyes I've *definitely* never seen. He backs me against a shelf of paper towels, his hands coming to rest on either side of my head as he stares at me.

"Hey," I breathe. I want to touch him. I want to run my greedy palms all over his body and climb him like tree. But I hold myself in check. Maybe I'm getting my wires crossed here.

"Why'd you kiss me on Saturday?" he asks in a gruff voice that makes my toes curl in my Louie Vuitton's.

I shrug. "Maggie wa—"

"Nope. Try again."

Val has never been bossy with me before and it is really working for me. I shift on my feet, then lick my lips. His eyes lock on my mouth and I release a shuddering breath. Tension builds to suffocating levels in the small room, and I can't take another second of it.

I launch myself at him, he stumbles into the shelf at his back with a soft grunt before my mouth is on his. He groans, his tongue twisting with mine as his thick fingers squeeze my hips and I wrap my arms around his neck, molding my body to his. I need him like I've never needed anything before. And I need him now.

"Val," I pant. "Need you."

"Oh, fuck, Bee," he mutters, his palms skating down my outer thighs to the hem of my skirt then rucking it up until it bunches at my waist.

When his fingers skate over the scrap of satin between my legs, I shudder and whimper into his throat, pressing wet kisses there. "Now Val." I drop my hands to his belt, unfastening it with quick fingers. A second later I have his hot cock in my palm and good god, it feels incredible to be touching him like this. He's thick and heavy and so ready for me.

I lift one foot to the lowest shelf behind him, opening myself to him. He groans again, then tugs my underwear to the side as I line his crown with my entrance. I'm soaked for him already and I don't waste a second urging him inside. I roll my hips and he thrusts forward, breaching my aching pussy.

A satisfied moan rips from my throat and his hands go to my ass, lifting me, he spins us around, so my back is against the shelving. Buried to the hilt, he slowly draws back, his feral gaze dipping to where we're joined. "Look Bee, watch my cock fill up your perfect pouty pussy," he demands.

Fuck yes, this is really working for me. I nod, dropping my eyes and the sight and sensations are so erotic, I clench around his length. He feels so good inside me, it's indescribable.

Valentine, my best friend in the whole world, is fucking me. And it's amazing.

His hips punch forward, then he slowly draws out again. Over and over, hard thrust, leisurely drag, hard thrust. My head rolls back on the shelf and I bite my lip to keep from screaming my pleasure. We're at work, for god's sake.

Soon he picks up his pace, delivering a punishing rhythm that sets my blood on fire and sends my body into euphoric bliss. I reach for his face, slide my fingers into the damp edges of his hair and smash my lips to his as I come on his thick dick.

"Fuck, fuck, fuck," he chants. "You're perfect Bee; so fucking perfect." Then he pulls out moments before coming in his fist.

I can't look away. I'm transfixed by the creamy

white liquid coating his fingers. I lick my lips, wondering how it would taste.

"Don't do that," he murmurs, tone deep and intoxicating.

My eyes dart up to his, and I smirk at the look he's giving me. "Why not?"

"Because then I'll be forced to feed it to you, and I don't have the time to fully appreciate the sight of my cum coating your pretty lips."

Shit, that's hot. How did I not know Val was a kinky fucker? I'm still trying to regulate my breathing but if he keeps talking like that, I'll be ready for round two and this is not the place. I clear my throat, fix my ruined underwear then wiggle my skirt back into position.

Val turns around and snatches a handful of paper towels from the shelf and cleans himself up before refastening his pants and belt. When his eyes meet mine again, I can barely breathe from the intensity of the emotions swirling in their depths.

"We need to talk," he says, caging me in once again.

I grin. "I'm pretty sure our bodies just did all our talking for us."

He shakes his head, a warm smile curving his lips as he tucks some errant strands of my long blonde hair behind my ear. "That might be, but I still want to hear the words. Every single one of them. Because once will never be enough for me. I've known it my whole life. So, we're going to talk about this, and we're going to figure a few things out."

Undiluted delight floods my entire body— because holy shit, this is really happening—but he's right. Of course, he's right. We need to talk about what we just did. And why the hell we did it at Hunters and Co., of all places while our dads and my sisters are in the middle of a meeting on the other side of the building.

"Tonight, at my place. I'll order in," I tell him.

He nods once. "It's a date." Then he leans in and takes my mouth in a seductively slow kiss that fries what's left of my brain cells.

I've just finished compiling the data on a skipper I know Snow will enjoy taking in when Dad steps out of his office and calls me. "Belle, can I have a minute?"

I collect the sheets I'd just printed out from the printer and tuck them into a fresh file. I bring it with me as I stride into Dad's domain. It's the only private office we have; the rest of us are scattered throughout the pit.

Taking a seat, I place the file on his desk and gesture to it with my chin. "Snow'll want this one," I tell him.

He picks it up, flips it open to the cover page I put together, then rolls his eyes. "Just make sure she doesn't go getting any ideas from this guy," he says, flicking it closed and handing it back to me.

I chuckle, "She already has ideas; you and I both know that."

Dad grumbles something under his breath about Snow being the death of him before shifting to sit back in his chair and eye me. "So, about our deal…"

I arch a brow. "What about it?"

He runs a hand through his salt and pepper hair. "We didn't discuss what I would get when I won. And now that I have, I want to collect. I'm just not sure what it is I'm collecting…"

"What you're collecting? What makes you think you've won?" I ask, trepidation thrumming in my veins.

"Look, I don't need to know more than I regrettably already do regarding you and Valentine. It's obvious that I've won. Everyone heard you two *working things out*, this morning."

Oh. My. Freaking. God. Please, please, just kill me now. Or you know, fake my death for me and I'll move to

Mexico and live off tacos and tequila for the rest of my days. Anything to get me out of this conversation.

"I'm pretty sure my offer prior to that date business was a neat grand. I'd be happy with that," Dad says, a haughty smirk on his arrogant face.

I stare at him. Why isn't he freaking out or having a meltdown? He just told me he heard me having sex. Which is horrifying. For both of us. "How are you acting so cool right now?"

"Today, unfortunately, wasn't the first time I've had the great misfortune of overhearing one of my daughters doing something I never, *ever*, wanted to hear," he says with a shudder.

Eww.

I cringe. "That's umm, unsettling."

"You're telling me," he agrees. "Anyway, I'll take cash, check, or direct deposit."

I glare at him. "You won't be getting a cent from me. Not yet anyway," I mumble the last bit.

His gaze turns deadly, and he sits forward in his chair, bringing his elbows to the edge of his desk. "Explain."

Crap, maybe I should have just given him the damn money. Clearing my throat, again, I tell him. "We didn't... umm... really discuss much this morning. Val's coming over tonight for the umm, talking portion of our... umm..." I wave my hand in the air searching for a word, any word that will end this mortifying conversation once and for all.

"I get it," Dad grumbles, squeezing his eyes shut. "You can pay up tomorrow, then."

My shoulders slump as relief sweeps through me, then I get to my feet and hightail it out of there without a backward glance.

Chapter Nine

Valentine

It took me two hours to decide if I should bring flowers for Belle tonight. In the end I hit up the farmers market on the outskirts of Shiloh Springs and picked up a fresh bouquet from the florist who runs a stall there. She put together a stunning arrangement with flowers sourced from local farms.

When I pull into Belle's drive, I'm not the slightest bit nervous. I thought I would be...was expecting to be. But all I feel is complete calm. Nothing has ever felt more right. She'd kill me if I said that out loud, the grammar Nazi that she is. I grin as I climb out of the car and head for her door.

She swings it open before I even get there. She's changed into a pair of jeans that hug her curves impeccably, and a lightweight pink sweater that hangs off one shoulder. Her hair is in a knot atop her head, and I know she probably spent at least fifteen minutes perfecting that artfully messy look.

When our eyes meet, everything else fades away. It's just her and me, and we're finally, fucking finally, exactly where we're supposed to be.

"Hey," she murmurs, her shiny pink painted lips pursing as they take in the bouquet in my hands. "You didn't need to get me flowers."

"Yeah, I did. These are the first of many to come," I tell her, stepping into her space, then brushing my lips over her flushed cheek.

"Thank you," she breathes. She takes a step back, welcoming me inside. "I ordered food, It'll be here in…" she glances at the clock on the wall behind me. "Forty-five."

"Works for me," I tell her, kicking off my shoes and putting them on the rack by the door before heading to the kitchen. I open the cupboard under the sink and pull out a vase, fill it with water, then put the flowers in. Spinning around, I find Belle watching me with her elbows propped on the counter, chin resting atop her hands. "What?" I ask.

She shrugs. "Is it weird that I never noticed before how you just *fit* here? You know my house, you know me, you just... fit."

I grin and shake my head. "Sometimes we deliberately don't see things we don't want to acknowledge. Now, where do you want these?" I ask, holding up the vase.

"The table, please."

Placing them in the center of her long dining table, I turn back to see she's wandering over to the couch. I follow her, taking the other end of the sofa when she sits. She swivels around to face me as she tucks her long legs underneath her.

"So, where do we start?" she asks.

"Saturday?" I hedge.

She scrunches up her nose and shakes her head. "No. How about last Monday..." she gives me a pointed look and I chuckle.

"All right, what do you want to know?"

"What were you trying to hide from me?"

Not exactly how I wanted to kick this off, but if it's as good a place as any I suppose. Clearing my throat, I throw an arm over the back of the couch and hook my ankle over my knee as I angle my body to face hers. "It was a story. You know I've always liked to dabble here and there."

The look she gives me says she knows it was much more than just a random story. I narrow my eyes. "What do you know?"

Her cheeks flush and she gnaws on her bottom lip. Christ, I love when she does that. It's sexy as fuck and makes it hard to concentrate on anything but her mouth.

"I might have seen a bit of it..."

"A bit?"

She nods, then averts her eyes. "So, if we're doing this, there's probably something I should come clean about..."

Ah, there's that nervousness I was waiting for.

"Okaaay," I drawl. She fidgets with her nails, and I reach out and take her hand. "Hey, whatever it is, I'm sure it's fine. Or it will be..."

"I hacked your computer," she blurts.

My eyes widen. "You what?"

Her panicked gaze swings to me and she grabs both my hands, holding tight. "I was curious, and I just couldn't let it go. I was having hot as hell dreams, and they wouldn't stop. Every night Val. I woke up sexually frustrated and my poor vibrator, I think I'm going to need a new one. I had no choice! Please forg—"

I swoop in and seal my mouth over hers to shut her up. My fingers slide into her hair as I cup her jaw in my palms and angle her face as I deepen the kiss. My tongue invades her mouth, and she moans, then reaches for the bottom of my shirt, tugging it up. I draw back only long enough to hook my finger in the back of the collar and dispose of it, and then I'm on her again.

Wait, no. Fuck. We need to talk first.

I sever the kiss, breathing heavily I force myself back to my side of the couch. "Sorr—actually I'm not sorry. But we do need to talk more before I get sidetracked by your body again."

Belle nods, her eyes glazed and a dopey grin curving her lips. I smirk, feeling pretty damn smug about putting that look on her face.

Focus horndog!

Right, talking. "Okay, so you hacked my computer. I guess that means you saw…"

Her grin widens. "Everything. You've been holding out on me, Val. You've got some serious writing chops. And those sex scenes." She fans herself. "*Fifty Shades*, eat your heart out."

Heat creeps up my neck. "Uh, thanks."

"Why have you never said anything to me about, well, any of it?" she asks in a soft voice.

I run my hands through my hair, needing to keep

them busy so I don't reach for her again. "How could I tell you? You've been my best friend for as long as I can remember. I couldn't risk fucking with that. You mean everything to me, Belle. Losing you isn't an option."

She nods. "I completely understand. I've had those exact thoughts myself."

My eyes search her face, desperate for answers. "What made you change your mind?"

With a heavy sigh she flops back and tugs a cushion into her lap. "Snow has been at me for god knows how long about our friendship. Every time she'd bring it up, I'd shut her down. In all the years we've spent together, you've never dropped so much as a hint that you were interested in more." She drags her bottom lip between her teeth and stares at her nails.

When her gaze returns to mine, her blue eyes are full of fire. "Then I walked in on everyone betting on us—even our dads, Val. Apparently, everyone but me could see it. When I started reading that manuscript, I couldn't wrap my head around why you were using our names. I know, talk about a dumb blonde moment," she says with a self-deprecating laugh.

I shake my head. "Bee—"

She holds up a hand. "Just let me finish, please."

"Okay." Whatever she needs, I'm here for it.

"Thank you. So, after I saw Maggie on Friday, there was no way I was letting you see that nutbag on your own. I figured I'd just be around in case you needed back up. The bitch is crazy, Val."

"No shit," I mutter.

"Anyway, when she put her hands on you, I don't know...I just, I lost it. I mean who does she think she is? You can't just attack someone because they don't want to date you. And I don't know if you noticed, but she was trying to assimilate my look. Which is going to take a hell of a lot more than some cheap hair extensions and a dress from Target, thank you very much."

I shouldn't find the scowl she's wearing cute, but I really, really, do. "I did notice, but it took me a minute. She even had blue contacts."

Belle shudders. "You followed through with pressing charges, right?"

"Sure did. And I filed a restraining order," I assure her.

"Thank god. The last thing I need is a cheap knock off running around trying to steal my man."

My chest fills with satisfaction at her words. "Your man, huh?"

Her brow lifts as she stares me down. "I said what I said. Got a problem with it?"

"Not-a-one." I grin, and she mirrors it.

"I think that covers all the talking points that needed to be covered, don't you?" she asks, pushing up onto her knees and climbing over the cushions to reach me. She settles on my lap, her thighs bracketing mine, and I curl my hands around her hips.

"Just one more thing," I tell her when her lips are just a breath away from mine.

"What's that?" she whispers.

"I love you," I murmur, our lips brushing with each word. "Always have, always will. Don't make me live without this again." She nods, her blue eyes shining bright, and I close the gap, kissing her softly. My fingertips trace up her spine until they're tangled in her hair at the base of her skull. "I love you, and I'm never letting you go."

VAL KISSES ME UNTIL I SEE STARS AND I HAVE TO plant my hands on his shoulders, pushing him back so I can take a few deep breaths. He chuckles, the sound rich and masculine. He makes me so incredibly happy my head spins. Or maybe that's the lack of oxygen?

Either way, I don't care. Val is mine. He loves me. He never wants to let me go. My heart sings, a reaction that's usually reserved for when I find the perfect shoes to complement my outfit. Or vice versa.

With his hands buried in my hair, Val tugs the strands lightly and it feels *ah-maz-ing*. Not in a sexual way, but in an *oh god, that's so relaxing* kind of way. "Do that again," I encourage.

He chuckles again, sending a swarm of butterflies into flight in my chest. I smile at him, and he brings his lips back to mine. We kiss for what feels like days, slow and lazy.

"I love you, too, you know," I tell him between soul binding kisses. "Always have, always will."

"Yeah, Bee, I know," he murmurs against my mouth. "Now shut up and kiss me some more. We've got years to make up for."

I'm about to do just that when the doorbell rings and Val's hands slide down to my waist, holding me in place when I try to stand from his lap.

"It's dinner; I'll be right back," I promise with a laugh, this time successfully making it to my feet.

His hand shoots out, grabbing mine and tugging

me back onto the couch beside him. "You aren't going anywhere looking like that," he says, pushing up to his feet.

"Looking like what?" I demand.

"Thoroughly fucked," he deadpans as he reaches for his crotch and rearranges things downstairs.

"Fine, but for the record, you don't look much better."

He smirks then strides to the front door shirtless and collects the food. Instead of returning to the couch, he takes the brown paper bag into the kitchen and places it inside the oven.

"What are you doing?"

"That'll keep it warm enough for now," he says on his way back to me.

"But I'm hungr—"

"So am I," he says, bending over and grabbing me by the waist, then tossing me over his shoulder. One of his arms wraps around my thighs, holding me in place as he turns to the hall and heads for my room.

Oh. Oh, I like this plan. Very much.

Epilogue
SIX MONTHS LATER...

Belle

THE ONLY THING THAT'S CHANGED SINCE VAL AND I became a couple is that we have more sleepovers. That, and we share the same bed when we do stay at the other's house. Oh, and clothing is optional.

The transition from friends to lovers was seamless and as of today, we've officially been more than best friends for six months. We've spent every moment of it making up for lost time and I'm not complaining about a second of it. Time well spent, if you ask me.

We mostly stay at my place since all my clothes and shoes are there. I'm slowly working on improving Val's wardrobe. But truth be told, I prefer him in as little clothing as possible, if any at all. A fact he takes advantage of often.

Half of his stuff has migrated to my house, and I cleared a few drawers and made some hanging space for him in my closet. Okay, so I just moved some stuff into the cupboard in the guestroom to make some space for him. Same thing.

Aside from his hamsters, Muffin and Phyllis, and the racoon, Rocky, that he swears adopted him and not the other way around, everything he needs is already here.

I figure if I can let Bosco have sleepovers—even after what he did to my emerald pair of Sarah Jessica Parker B Pearl Sling Back Pumps—I can handle a couple of tiny hamsters and a weirdly domesticated raccoon moving in.

So, tonight, I'm going to pop the question. Who cares if we skip the moving in step? We're practically already living together.

"Kline, if you drop that chaise, I swear to god, I'll turn you into a eunuch," I threaten.

He rolls his eyes. "Don't get your panties in a wad; it slipped."

I glare at him as he passes me on his way into

Val's house. I want everything to be perfect when Val gets home. He's been away for the last five days on an out of state retrieval with his dad and Terrance, a bounty hunter who works with us on and off. I've missed him more than I thought possible.

Thank the technology gods for video calls. I've been singing their praises all week. Phone sex is *so* much better when you can actually see your partner. A dreamy smile tips my lips as I think about last night's call...

"Eww, knock that shit off," Snow grouses.

"What?"

She rolls her eyes. "You get this weird look on your face when you're thinking dirty thoughts about Val. It's gross; he's like our brother."

I scoff and cross my arms. "As if I'd do the things I do to Val to my brother."

"Jesus H. Christ I wish you girls would censor yourselves when I'm around," Dad grumbles, sidestepping us as he carries a bag full of candles inside.

"Sorry, not sorry," I call after him.

He mutters something unintelligible as he goes about his business, and Snow and I burst out laughing.

By the time I hear Val's truck pull into the driveway, everything is ready. Soft vanilla and honey scented candles light every available surface, a gourmet platter along with a bottle of champaign and two flutes sit waiting on a small side table, and I am sprawled out across a black velvet chaise lounge in his favorite baby pink, lace lingerie set. And, of course, a pair of matching killer heels I got just for the occasion.

Anticipation thrums wild in my veins as the click of his key in the lock echoes through the house. He swings the door open, dropping his duffle in the entry as he steps inside. I watch as his head swings from one side of the room to the other, taking in the scene before him. I may have also had all his furniture moved to the shed out back to clear the way for my vision to come to life.

When his gaze finally lands on me, heat flares in his eyes. He wastes no time in kicking the door closed behind him and making his approach. "To what do I owe the pleasure of all this?" he asks.

I lick my lips, then slide off the chaise, coming to rest on my knees before him. I take his hands in mine, peering up into his loving eyes, and I have no doubts.

"Valentine Foster, you've been my best friend through all the very best and worst moments of my life. I can share my passions, my fears, and my dreams with you. I respect and adore absolutely everything about you. You fill my soul with peace and love, and I don't want to ever live another day without you at my side. Val, will you marry me?"

He stares down at me, jaw working as he swallows hard and shakes his head. "You couldn't wait just another week, could you?" he murmurs, a smile finally emerging on his scruff covered face.

And that is not the response I was expecting. I tilt my head. "Is that a no?"

"Of course not. And no take backs!" he says, dropping to his knees with me. Our hands still clasped, he leans in and brushes a kiss to each of my cheeks, then my forehead. "I love you, Bee, and I want to marry you more than anything. So much so, I was planning to ask you..." he levels me with an exasperated frown. "I had it all planned out. Flowers, music, a romantic setting—"

"You snooze, you lose," I say, shuffling closer so I can wrap my arms around his neck. Our foreheads touch, and I smile up into his beautiful eyes. "You can still do it. No point wasting all that effort."

He chuckles. "Nah, I like your idea *way* better," he says, kissing me again as his palms skate up and down my sides, sending a shiver down my spine. He grins against my mouth. "So, is that chaise ours now or did you hire it special for the occasion?"

I smirk. "It's ours."

"Excellent," he murmurs. "I was hoping you'd say that."

"Oh?"

His hands stop their torturous glide along my sensitive flesh at my hips, where he grips them before lifting me and placing my butt on the edge of the chaise. When his lusty gaze locks on mine, I know without a doubt, I'm going to enjoy everything that comes next.

THE END

Also by JB Heller

SHILOH SPRINGS WORLD

HUNTERS & CO. SERIES

Catastrophe Magnet

Hacker Heart

Red Hot Rebel (2023)

Poker Face (2023)

BROKEN BOYS SERIES

Broken Boys Break Hearts

Broken Boys Fight Harder

Broken Boys Despise Deceit

Broken Boys Crave Chaos

STANDALONE

What If It's Right?

ROM COMS

UNEXPECTED LOVERS SERIES

Complete Series

The Starfish Method

The Covert Cam Girl

The Unexpected Manny

The Ballbuster's Dilemma

Falling For His Fake Fiancé

Wooing His Accidental Wife

AWKWARD GIRLS SERIES

Complete Aussie Series

Pink Bits

Llama Drama

Fertile Myrtle

ROMANTIC SUSPENSE

ATTRACTION SERIES

Complete Series

Undeniable Attraction

Pure Attraction

Fierce Attraction

Morgan Sisters Duo (Prequel)

ALPHA ONE PROTECTION SERIES

(Attraction Series Spin Off)

Worth The Risk

Worth The Wait

JB Heller is an average Aussie housewife and Mumma in her mid 30's with a wicked sexy imagination.

These days she writes mostly romantic comedies, drawing inspiration from her everyday life.

Monday to Friday you can find JB glued to her laptop weaving words or trolling Pinterest for her next potential muse. Come the weekend, it's family time. (And of course lots of reading and Netflix binges.)

Want to know more?

Website: jbtheindie.com
Facebook Reader Group: Heller's Bookwhorders